Pinch Canyon
4:18 P.M.

The pain was unbelievable. Danna honestly could not believe that anything could hurt so much. She could not believe that she, Danna Press, *she* was a burden. She was the kind of person who did everything right the first time. Now she was nothing but a nuisance, a jerk who had to be carried?

And Beau — what was he doing? She couldn't see from here. She screamed, "What is he doing, Hall? Don't let him, Hall! Make him come with us."

It was hard to think through the pain.

But she would rather have pain than be held responsible for Beau's death. How could Beau be so selfish, so crazy? How dare he put them in this position?

Running back into the fire....

FLASH FIRE

Caroline B. Cooney

SCHOLASTIC INC.
New York   Toronto   London   Auckland   Sydney

No part of this publication may be reproduced in whole or in part, or stored in a retrieval system, or transmitted in any form or by any means, electronic, mechanical, photocopying, recording, or otherwise, without written permission of the publisher. For information regarding permission, write to Scholastic Inc., 555 Broadway, New York, NY 10012.

ISBN 0-590-48496-6

12 11 10 9 8 7 6 5 4 3 2 1   9   6 7 8 9/9 0 1/0

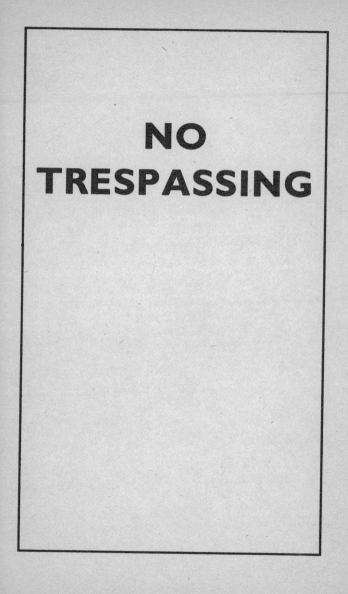

NO
TRESPASSING

Pinch Canyon
Wednesday, October 27th
the Press house
3:15 P.M.

ROCK SLIDE AREA
RESIDENTS ONLY
NO OUTLET
ARSON WATCH
ABSOLUTELY NO SMOKING
NO TRESPASSING
ARMED RESPONSE

A stranger who drove into Pinch Canyon would think he was entering a war zone. Danna herself would have removed the signs lining the road, and opted to *have* rock slides, strangers, trespassing, and, of course, armed response.

ARMED RESPONSE was Danna's personal favorite. She had never seen an ARMED RESPONSE, but she remained hopeful. Someday, uniformed responders carrying submachine guns and leading slavering dogs would vault out of a camouflage vehicle and surround one of the houses.

With her luck, she'd be in school.

Danna Press wanted action. Her very own mother and father had just entered a twelve-step serenity class. Please. Who would want serenity?

Danna felt she was an ideal candidate for a kidnapping. She could at least witness a major crime, and then have to testify in court, or else provide vital information about an assassination attempt on the President.

Why, Danna wanted to know, could she not be a terrorist, or date one?

When earthquakes struck, why wasn't it *her* house that got lifted from its foundations and tumbled down down down into the treacherous canyon below? That way, television cameras would focus upon the Press family, the nation aching over their plight, and falling in love with the beauteous Danna.

But no. The Press family continued on its placid way, outgrowing jeans and renting movies.

Danna turned on the TV for company. Los Angeles (not her area, of course; she couldn't be that lucky) was engulfed in flames for the ninth day in a row. People are packing their Volvos with photograph albums, thought Danna, calling the dog, hosing down the roof, rescuing their neighbors. And what am I doing? Vocabulary.

"A conflagration!" said the reporter eagerly. Now *there* was a vocabulary word.

Danna studied the TV map. Nothing in the way of a conflagration was near Pinch Canyon. She watched the people watching fires. People had driven to freeway overpasses and brought binoculars and even lawn chairs from which to enjoy the fires at a comfortable distance. Since neither Danna nor her brother, Hall, was old enough to drive, and since their mom and dad checked on them about every sixty seconds, this was not going to be a possibility. They were stuck on Pinch.

Pinch Canyon, well named, was a slot in the mountains, as thin and vertical as a toaster waiting for bread. Twisted oaks and shrubs dusty with heat and lack of rain filled the narrow box bottom on both sides of Pinch Canyon Road. The south rockface flared almost straight up. It was the kind of rock that peeled itself off in layers after storms. Dangerous, impossible-to-climb rock, scarred by years of erosion.

The north face was where the houses had been built. Twenty-one houses were pasted on the canyon's few slanting meadows. Driveways curled as tight and steep as spirals on school notebooks. Swimming pools and tennis courts and paddocks for horses had been carved into the hillsides.

Most people shared a driveway. Three houses peeled off theirs: At the bottom was Danna's, Mr. and Mrs. Luu lived in the middle, and stacked on top of them, the Aszlings. Everybody had a lot of land, but it was mainly vertical.

Pinch Canyon had no outlet. The road turned sharply off Grass Canyon Road, was blocked a quarter mile in by a gate, and then cut another mile and a half to stop dead at the foot of Pinch

Mountain. Pinch Mountain looked like a five-hundred-foot sphinx glaring down the road, its huge paws forming the sides of the canyon. Most hills around LA were rounded, but her own personal canyon was sharp and harsh, the sides dropping roughly — fifty feet here, a hundred feet there.

On television, a large stucco house, built in pastel stacks like huge children's blocks, slowly caught fire. Smoke came before flames, so first the house turned into a soot-breathing dragon. Then, magnificent and horrific, it turned blazing gold. In minutes, only its black skeleton remained.

"You guys get all the good stuff," Danna said to the television. "I'm stuck here with abdicate and abjure."

Vocabulary ought to stay in elementary school. Sixth grade was the absolute oldest you should have to have vocabulary. Ninth grade was far too sophisticated for vocabulary lists. Nevertheless, she had a vocabulary list, one of those tricky ones meant to catch you by the alphabet heels. Abdicate, abjure, abhorrent, aborigine, and abstention.

Although Mom and Dad were at the studio today, fighting over a contract, they kept relentlessly in touch. There was no avoiding the family rule of Homework First. What with beepers, E-mail, fax, and phone, Danna and Hall never had a minute of freedom. Mom even wore a wristwatch that beeped at appropriate intervals to remind her to check on Danna's homework/clarinet practice/dance practice/tennis practice/horseback riding.

I'm sick of vocabulary, thought Danna, who sickened quickly over most homework.

She could go outside and swim with her brother, but the temperature was in the nineties and the Santa Ana wind was no relief: It cleaned out the lungs like a dry scouring pad. Because of the fires, the air was full of ash. Strange, particulate black ash. Not papery flakes, but little microscopic pieces of things, each different, like snowflakes — as if, with a microscope, you would know that one was from a roof shingle, another from a baby crib, or a birdhouse.

Anyway, Danna was wearing her favorite T-shirt, which was white, and she didn't want it to turn gray from the falling ash. It was from the Los Angeles County Coroner's office, featuring the outline of a human body, as if chalked by police on a street. It came down to her knees, making the chalk body about a quarter life-size. Mom and Dad said it was sick and tasteless, but since writing sick and tasteless screenplays was their trade, they had to quit arguing early. Danna always got a kick out of the fact that her strict, careful, and affectionate parents wrote stuff so sick that when it finally came on television, Danna and Hall weren't even allowed to see it.

"So okay," said Danna to the television, "I should feel sorry for the owners of that burned-up house, and their children, and their pets, and their insurance company, and I do, I really do. I really am a nice person and I do feel sorry when other people suffer. It's just that nothing happens to *me*."

Danna planned what she would take if she had to run from a fire.

Kittens first.

The stray cat she'd adopted had provided kittens. Everybody who walked into the house fell in love with the kittens, crooning and cuddling, but not a single kitten-adorer would actually take one home. The mama cat moved on and left all seven babies to Danna. Danna named the kittens for LA burbs, so they had Pasadena, Burbank, Venice, LAX for the airport, and so forth. Her brother thought this was pretty crummy, a kitten named LAX, so he was calling the kittens by the names of fruit trees that grew on their property: Orange, Lemon, Kumquat, etc. Since the kittens looked alike, you couldn't tell which you were calling anyway, and Kumquat (or LAX) and Lemon (or Venice) just skittered around between your shoes trying to get you to fall over on one of their brothers or sisters.

Danna couldn't even guarantee there were seven kittens anymore, because getting them in one place at one time, even for meals, wasn't a happening thing.

Even though the fire was miles away, and would have to work its way through thousands of houses, cross major highways, step over hundreds of firefighters, and outwit dozens of tanker planes before it hit Pinch Canyon, Danna entertained herself by making kitten contingency plans.

the brushfire
3:16 P.M.

Five miles up Grass Canyon Road, and down a minor road that led inland and north of Pinch Canyon, was an ordinary brush fire. It moved along casually, like a person bored with exercise.

What you wanted to do with fire was to kill it around the edges. The edge was its line of attack. So you put your trucks and your firefighters at the edge. You bottled the fire up until it ate the fuel and then the fire died.

A small troop of firefighters used long-handled Pulaskis, a sort of combination hoe and axe, to rip up the spiky brown underbrush, chain saws to take down trees, and shovels to turn dirt on top of this tinder and take away its oxygen. Everybody was a little bored, because the really neat fires were elsewhere, and they were stuck on shovel duty.

They paused now and then to sip water from canteens or Cokes from cans.

At this particular minute, they thought they were in charge.

The fire knew otherwise.

the Press house
3:20 P.M.

Hall wasn't swimming, just floating. From the air, their pool wasn't turquoise like everybody else's, but dark and secret because the tile that lined the Press pool was deep green. They'd bought the house by helicopter, flying over to make sure of the neighborhood, so Hall knew exactly what it looked like from the sky.

There was a lot of air traffic today. Silver-and-red tanker planes skimmed Pinch Mountain, headed for distant fires to dump their gooey loads of red fire retardant on endangered hillsides. Bucket-fitted helicopters flew to the Pacific, filled up with salt water, and rotored loudly back to pour water on roofs or yards. The copters were white with yellow tails and red-and-white-striped propellers, giving them the look of children's toys that actually flew.

It was a good day to float on your back and check out the sky.

Of course, the air was a little tough to breathe. Hall might as well have asthma. Every now and then, he had to go vertical, treading water and coughing.

Halstead Press loved the interval in his day that came after school and before dinner. This was when he felt most like a Californian: hot and tanned and timeless. No minutes. No hours. Just the moment.

Above the Press property, the immense Luu deck launched itself toward the Pacific Ocean. The last mud slide had taken away a good deal of the Luu property. Where once there had been a steep hillside, there was now a vertical drop. Mr. and Mrs. Luu had covered the bare dirt with huge blue plastic tarps, so if it rained again, the dirt wouldn't get wet and slide out from under the entire house. The tarp was weighted down with sandbags so it couldn't blow away, and the sandbags themselves were linked by heavy ropes, so they couldn't fall to the bottom of Pinch Canyon. It was a long way, and would be a very unpleasant fall, even for a sandbag.

Hall loved to swing himself up onto their deck (when they weren't home to know about it) by the sandbag ropes.

It was stunt man stuff and Danna filmed him every time. They planned to show the films to their parents in ten or twenty years when they were too old for their parents to punish them.

There were no gentle meadows around Pinch Canyon. You couldn't run up these hills. You had to crawl, or go sideways, and hang onto things. Naturally Hall crawled up the hills all the time, and slipped, and dislodged dead roots, and ruined his clothes. Once Hall asked Mr. Luu if he was worried about the mud or the fires.

"Halstead, my man," said Mr. Luu, who loved Hall's name, and said it was destined for a bronze plaque on a very important door, "what's to worry? If there's a fire, we rebuild. If there's a mud slide, we sandbag. And if we have to start over, then we do."

"Besides," said Mrs. Luu, "I want to redecorate anyway."

Above the Luu house were the Aszlings. Where the Luus had wedged in a stable and paddock, and the Presses had decided on tennis courts, the Aszlings had chosen garages. Their land was so steep that even the garages were terraced. The driveway split like fingers, so each of the four cars had its own smaller, steeper driveway. They had of course remote control for the garage doors, and their Jaguars slipped in and out, black and sleek and secretive as the jungle animal.

Mr. Aszling was in aerospace and Mrs. Aszling was in computers. They gave parties all the time and skied at their mountain place and traveled to the Far East and now and then even remembered Geoffrey.

Mr. and Mrs. Aszling had never had children but apparently always wanted them, and a year ago adopted a little boy from a Bucharest orphanage. It was all very exciting, but the little boy proved difficult. Perhaps nobody had hugged him enough in Romania, or even hugged him at all. Perhaps nobody had spoken to him, or let him be with other children, or eat a meal at a table. Geoffrey was just a silent little animal. He didn't improve much. He was not rewarding. The fun had gone out of the adoption, and if you could un-adopt, the Aszlings would have done it.

Hall loved Geoffrey Aszling.

There was something proud and brave in this solemn little boy that Hall respected so much. Inside Geoffrey were tortures and terrors. If you could see his soul, you would see a hillside ravaged and bare like the mountain, as if the color of Geoffrey's babyhood were sun-baked mud.

If he sat quietly with Geoffrey, and waited longer than Hall could wait for anything else on earth, Geoffrey would approach him. It was like feeding a wild bird. If every day you extended your palm with the sunflower seeds, eventually it would sit on your finger to eat out of your hand.

He'd been reading up on childhood emotional disorders and gotten interested in autism. Geoffrey did not have this dreadful syndrome, but there was a similarity. Hall cared intensely about Geoffrey's inability to love and to be loved.

Hall's family was very huggy. Whenever anybody went anywhere, they hugged. Not just a passing touch, but a bear hug. Dad still kissed him good night. Mom liked to stand behind him and massage his shoulder blades and kiss the back of his neck. Hall knew that he and Danna had the original prototype Super Parents, and he couldn't stand it that twice now Geoffrey had lost the parent lottery.

Hall knew, through Geoffrey, that he wanted to work with damaged little kids. Kids who had been hit, or hurt, or endured war or slaughter or abandonment.

He also knew that it wouldn't pay anything, and his parents would have little use for a career that paid nothing. Secrets were funny things. With some guys, the secrets they kept from their parents were drugs, or drinking, or being gay. Hall's secret was how much he wanted to help the Geoffreys of the world.

Yesterday, he'd leaned on the Aszlings' bell until the maid answered. (He never knew these maids; they were never the same woman; perhaps they sent their cousins to work when they were sick of housecleaning; or perhaps the Aszling household was regarded as an entrée for all illegals of a particular South American town, and everybody took turns scrubbing the Aszlings' bathrooms or pruning their bushes.) Anyway, Hall ran in yelling "So, Geoffrey, my man, how was your day?" and Geoffrey, who liked to speak a single word alternate months, yelled back, "Hall, my man!"

Hall felt like a million dollars. He returned home triumphant, yearning to share this huge victory with somebody, but his parents thought Geoffrey was creepy, and they didn't like their fifteen-year-old son hanging out with a four-year-old, even though at the same time they were mad at the Aszlings for giving up and proud of Hall for bothering.

Intellectually, Halstead Press knew that fire raged in twelve different places around Los Angeles, but Hall was a person who thought about people, not events. He floated on his back, staring at a sky that was normally blue, shading his eyes to keep the ash out, and planning Geoffrey's progress.

the brushfire
3:21 P.M.

Fire creates its own weather.

Around the firefighters up Grass Canyon, the wind became an invisible vortex, getting hotter and hotter, swifter and swifter. It had just become a tornado that nobody could see.

Without warning — or at least any warning the firefighters saw — the heat sucked the flames skyward, into a sudden horrific wall of flame.

It's one thing to fight a fire around your ankles.

It's quite another to fight a fire a hundred feet tall.

The rules and the hope changed in half a minute.

They stopped trying to fight it.

They practiced staying alive until it moved on.

the Aszling house
3:23 P.M.

Of course Elony wasn't allowed to smoke in the house. Mr. and Mrs. Aszling regarded cigarettes like an invasion of gangs bent on murder. Let her light up a cigarette and they'd be in there shrieking and fanning the air and shooing her outside.

Elony loved smoking.

You couldn't tell her it wasn't fun. It felt good, it gave you energy, it was your own private pleasure, and if she had to give up Spanish, she sure wasn't giving up cigarettes.

She stepped outside to have a cigarette. Elony flinched at the heat. She could hardly believe it was this hot. She felt a creepy prickle on her skin, as if she were freezing in the heat. These fires. It was awful, what was happening to this beautiful beautiful city.

Elony loved LA. It was so full of itself. She loved being part of the huge event that was LA: the huge event of everybody doing better. Elony was going to do better, too. She was going to get rich and drive a car and buy beautiful clothing that fit.

The key, she had decided, was reading. The big gap between her and the Anglos wasn't skin and wasn't green cards and wasn't height and wasn't even language.

The big gap was that they could read and she could not.

Elony was fighting her way toward reading, without the slightest idea how. There had been no school in her lifetime in her village. She had come to the conclusion that she had to get English inside her mind, not just on her lips. Today she would start thinking in English. All other thoughts she would push out of her mind.

It was killing her.

It made her blink and flinch and frown and twitch. Strangers must think she was getting a disease.

I am, she thought. English.

One entire side of the vast Aszling house was glass doors. A door cracked, enough for a head to poke out, but not enough to let the air-conditioning out. Elony had just washed every single one of those immense panes of glass, inside and out. She let smoke slowly leave her lungs as Chiffon's sneaky little eyes checked her over. Chiffon was Baby Geoffrey's nurse, not that Chiffon had ever once made the slightest effort to do a single thing with Geoffrey other than be sure he didn't drown in the pool.

"I'm going out for a while, Elony," called the Anglo girl, car keys in her hand. Chiffon was pretty in the borderline way that meant she thought more of her looks than other people did. She was probably going to have her nails done, or her hair. She was always taking a key to the best car the Aszlings had not driven that day, and going off on errands. Hers, not the Aszlings.

Elony tapped her watch. "Bus," she shouted

at Chiffon. "You stay. I go." Elony had a two-
hour bus ride down Grass Canyon, down the
Pacific Coast Highway, and finally into LA.
Sometimes the bus's air-conditioning worked
and sometimes it didn't. Elony had exactly two
more minutes left in her work day, and then she
had to hustle down Pinch Canyon Road to get
the bus at Grass Canyon.

"You can stay late, Elony," explained Chiffon,
since Elony's life and plans didn't matter. "I
have to do this stuff, it's important. I'll be back
in an hour or two." Chiffon waved, as if a flick
of the wrist made everything okay, and darted
off.

"No, you stay!" shouted Elony. She raced back
into the house after Chiffon, chasing her
through the huge rooms and up the occasional
wide flat step that divided one space from another. Elony hated how she didn't have enough
English to go around for situations like this.

But Chiffon had had too much of a head start.
Giggling triumphantly, Chiffon waved and
drove off.

I hate you! thought Elony.

No cigarette would make her feel better about
missing the bus. What was she supposed to do
now? Leave the little boy alone in the house?
The maddening thing was that Mr. or Mrs. Aszling would care only if somebody found out.
They just wanted to *look* like good parents.

Nobody would pay her overtime for staying

with Geoffrey. She had found out that Mrs. Aszling was breaking laws by paying her so little.
She also knew if she mentioned it, Mrs. Aszling
would fire her. If Elony missed the bus, one of
them would have to drive her home. She knew
from experience that instead of thanking her for
staying with Geoffrey, they'd just be mad about
the long drive.

Mr. and Mrs. Aszling had not bothered to learn
how to pronounce her name. They never talked
to her. Never asked any questions. Never said,
"How did you get to the States, Elony?"

So she'd never told them about the civil war
she had survived, the brutal hike over mountains, the fording of a river full of disease and
corpses. How she had paid for that border crossing in a stinking airless truck: with her body.
They never even asked how old she was.

Seventeen.

Here in America, seventeen-year-olds were
still children. Not Elony. Elony scrubbed toilets,
mopped floors, polished furniture, and ironed
more clothing every week than her entire village
had possessed.

The baby is not my responsibility, thought
Elony, furiously stubbing out the cigarette. He's
Chiffon's.

Elony didn't look in on Geoffrey. He would
be exactly where Chiffon had left him, curled
on floor pillows, sucking his thumb, watching
for the zillionth time a tape of *Cops*. Geoffrey

loved *Cops* as long as he was safely wrapped in his blankie.

The blankie drove Mr. and Mrs. Aszling wild.

It was three yards of velour, a gaudy vivid fuschia purple, from which Elony had meant to sew a bathrobe for herself, until Geoffrey adopted it. Geoffrey didn't like to meet strangers without his velour. Mr. and Mrs. Aszling never suggested repaying Elony for the cloth.

Geoffrey never moves anyway, she told herself. He'll be fine. He'll just lie there in his blankie.

Elony got her purse, an immense black carrier in which she kept her entire life, and left the house. At the top of the four-fingered Aszling driveway, in the shade of the thick pines, she lit another cigarette. In this appalling heat, shade made no difference whatsoever. Hurrying down the steep switchbacks, she passed the paddock behind the Luu house, where the two horses always frightened her, and then the Press house. It hurt her ankles to go downhill because it was so steep.

Down on Pinch Canyon Road, half hidden by the two-story green exclamation points of cypress trees, were Mexican yardmen waving, but not at Elony. They were hoping to get a ride with the Severyn boy, who usually obliged anybody fortunate enough to be in the right place at the right time.

Elony hurried, so as to be in the right place at the right time.

the Severyn house
3:25 *P.M.*

Beau Severyn was bored.

Everything about life and school bored him these days. He didn't want to be bothered. His parents regarded boredom as failure: It meant you weren't disciplined enough, or trying hard enough.

LaLa Land, they called this place. To Beau, "la la" meant frothy people who never stopped to think. Beau had never met anybody like that in Los Angeles. This was the thinking-est crowd on earth: how to get ahead, how to mold a better body, how to have a better relationship, how to score, earn, fight, win, get published, be a star.

Beau phoned his father at work, although Dad didn't like him to do that. Dad was in charge of network news advertising. Companies didn't like sponsoring disasters; they yanked their ads when the news was race riots or celebrity murder trials or baseball strikes or, in this case, fire. Dad was a wreck over the fires, but it wasn't the fires wrecking him; it was advertisers whimpering their way out of contracts. Dad was losing millions and he was ulcerated and crazed. "Yes, Beau, what is it?" snapped his father, implying that it had better be good. His father had no use for people, especially sons, who were not the best.

"Dad, the television says the fires are getting a little closer." It was not the fires that worried

Beau and it was not the fires he wanted his father
to talk about. But he and his father did not have
intimate conversations, or even conversations,
and he could only recite, as his father did, the
news.

"What did I tell you last night, Beau? Pinch
Mountain is a firebreak. That little brush fire
last year burned every twig. The whole wilderness back there is naked as a baby. In any event,
the fires are miles away." His father's voice was
raspy and tense.

Beau knew his father wanted a cigarette. Giving up smoking was killing Dad. He'd be better
off risking lung cancer than getting this frantic.
But Beau didn't say so. Mom acted as if the most
important thing in the history of time was Dad
quitting cigarettes. When Dad took a deep deep
breath Beau could hear through the phone, it
wasn't Dad schooling himself to be patient with
his son; it was a pretend lungful of friendly calm-
ing wonderful smoke.

"Dad," said Beau, who had been up on that
mountain with Halstead Press, fooling around,
and knew that the result of last year's minor fire
was that the undergrowth this year was stronger
and fuller than ever, "the mayor is ordering evac-
uations — "

"Miles from you!" snapped his father. "What
are you really asking me, David?"

David was his real name. Mom and Dad used
it only in anger, never in love. It gave Beau the

creeps, as if his real name were poisoned now and could never be used.

Beau avoided the topic of what he was really asking, just as the entire family had avoided it for so long. "If we had to evacuate the house," he said finally, "what should we save? I mean — "

He meant the box. The dumb stupid box on the mantelpiece that he thought about all the time now.

"Beau, your mother and I do not worry about earthquakes or fires. We take our chances. The odds are in our favor." Beau's parents did not approve of worry. If you had enough self-discipline and paid enough attention to the details, you could dispense with worry. Therefore it was against the rules for Beau to say that his life was evenly divided between boredom and worry.

"I know, Dad. I guess, just in case, I was trying to work out — "

"If something goes wrong, Beau, I have faith in you. You'll handle things. Now listen, I'm in a meeting."

Beau hung up slowly and surveyed his house. Twelve thousand square feet, enough for a high school in some parts of the world. Each time the network paid his father more, his parents bought more house and more car to match. Beau loved the sheer size of it — room after room after room, each a great spread of cool tile floor the color of sliced cucumber. Glass walls illuminated the dusty olive California hills and the indigo sky, backlit with California sun.

Except now, of course, when it was backlit by distant fires.

Outside, oak and pine, oleander and cypress leaned against each other, their branches and scents interwoven. A reflecting pool filled the huge atrium, while the lap pool lined the highest part of the property like a canal.

There were not many houses on Pinch Canyon because there were not many building sites. The Severyns had the most beautiful spot of all, said his mother, and although Beau did not agree with his mother on much, he agreed with her on that.

Beau went outside to check garden hoses. If fire came, he didn't care how much danger there was nor how foolhardy it might be: He was staying with the house. It made him feel wide-chested and great-hearted to make that resolution. He rather hoped he would have to defend his property, with a great blazing enemy to stave off.

The two maids and the two groundskeepers were leaving. The Mexicans paused, hoping Beau would drive them down to the bus stop. They didn't want to walk in this heat. The bus would pick them up on Grass Canyon Road, and two miles down Grass the road would intersect with the Pacific Coast Highway. From there they would sit stolidly for however long it took to reach their Los Angeles neighborhood.

It would have been impossible to live the way Pinch Canyon did and not have household help. What with careers and shopping, luncheon dates and fashion decisions, body sculpting and aromatherapy and relationship discussion, who had time to cook or clean? Beau's parents had no idea what a household chore was and certainly never expected their children to do one. They could not imagine washing their own car or doing their own laundry. Beau's mother would no sooner contribute to a school bake sale than swim in a storm drain.

His parents were fond of their children, but on the side. Like a sauce they might not want once they tasted it.

Halstead and Danna Press referred to their parents as SuperMom and SuperDad. Beau privately referred to his as SemiDad and NeverMom. He liked them. If he, too, were a grown-up, he'd enjoy their company and be friends. But they were not actually parents in any sense. They were beautiful, rich people who maintained a beautiful house in which they kept children who had better be beautiful, too.

Poor Elisabeth did not meet the guidelines. Last week, Beau's mother lamented to her women friends, "How could Aden and I, of all people, turn out a knock-kneed, nearsighted, overweight, boring little girl?"

"Mom, don't talk like that about Elisabeth," said Beau afterward. "Lighten up. She's only eight. Give her time."

"Beau, darling, these are my friends. They understand. I need understanding. You don't know how difficult it is, a daughter like that. Let me describe to you what I had in mind."

Elisabeth was never going to be what Mom had in mind.

"Would you like a ride to the bus stop?" Beau asked the help.

They nodded. There were never conversations with the help, just orders and nods.

"Wanna play tennis?" he asked his sister on the way to the garage. Tennis was an essential skill in their circle. He was always trying to tutor Elisabeth in the essentials.

"You'll beat me." Elisabeth invariably took that view: Why do anything; somebody will beat me. Mom of course hated having a daughter so lacking in drive and self-discipline.

"You need practice, Lizzie. I'll be back in five minutes."

Beau took the Suburban. His parents had bought it on a whim, immediately hated it and never touched it again. Everybody else had bought English: Land Rover or Range Rover. Beau loved the Suburban. With room to ferry a small band and its equipment, or else half a sports team, it was high off the road, heavy but easy to maneuver, and the driver had a great view and tons of power.

He picked up two more yardmen trudging down Pinch, and honked as he approached the gate so he wouldn't have to slow down. The guard was poky opening up, and Beau had to come to a full stop. He made sure to glare at the guy to let him know he'd better not cause this problem on Beau's return.

Grass Canyon Road
3:30 *P.M.*

Matt Marsh was the happiest, most excited twenty-two-year-old in the great state of California.

It was the big game. And he was on the team.

He was wearing a new helmet, since the old one had melted fighting yesterday's Altadena fire, and he was using, of course, a new hose, since the one he had held to save his own life had also melted.

Matt referred to the fires in sports terms: The score, for example was: 100,000 acres burned, 240 houses destroyed, 44 casualties, no deaths.

In some weird way, Matt was cheering for the fire.

He was awed by it. Stunned by it. Fascinated by it. They were fighting it hard and relentlessly, and yet it was winning: Winning so brilliantly, he could only admire it. It was like getting beaten by the world champion: There was a certain valor even in defeat.

He was gleeful about his army's numbers: 85

engines, 30 bulldozers, 31 water tenders, 8 aerial bombers, 7 helicopters.

And one huge awesome spectacular lethal fire.

And that was just Grass Canyon! There were another ten or so fires elsewhere. Matt, like most of the firefighters, was mutual aiding. Each town offered its services and equipment to the neighborhood that needed them most. Matt, however, knew this part of LA well: He'd grown up a few miles south of here, in Pinch Canyon.

Command knew that Grass would be tough to defend. Where there were houses, of course, people soaked lawns at night with sprinklers, and so the gardens and grass were green and lush and somewhat damp. But above the houses, Grass Canyon rose rather gently to three- and four-hundred-foot heights, covered by shrubby, weedy growth that was thick, sturdy, and very very dry. Previous fires had not touched it. Mud had not slid down it. Grass Canyon was just thousands of acres of tinder.

Therefore, the critical objective was to hold the fire north of the wide asphalt break of the road itself.

They did not have a hope of actually putting the approaching fire out. It was mammoth and many sided, driven by maddened wind. The fire was not neat. It zigged, it hopscotched, it doubled back. There were few places actually to set up lines of defense.

Bulldozer teams were hitting the west, seaward, flank of the fire, to keep it out of the adjoining urban areas.

The only thing June's crew could do was try to save houses and lives.

"Great," said June sarcastically. She was his captain. The first woman in this fire department, she'd gone through a lot. She was medium in every way: medium high, medium wide, medium looks — but first in guts. "I see four more jerks up on roofs with their garden hoses. What do you bet we get to that hydrant on top of the hill and there's no water pressure? They've sucked it all up."

The newest trend — wet roofs. What did they think they were accomplishing? If they'd kept brush away from the house and had a tile roof instead of wood shingle, they'd have a prayer. But all they were now, these roof-wetters, were jerks.

In fact, this neighborhood looked as if the Homeowners' Association had said: "Be sure to collect logs, pieces of plywood you might need someday, bales of hay and, of course, full gasoline cans. That way when the fire comes, your house will *really* explode."

"Listen, buddy," shouted Matt, "you need to get out of here."

"My house is my life," shouted the man right back.

"Life is life," said Matt. "Houses are houses."

This sounded profound to Matt, but it

sounded stupid to the homeowner, who made a rude gesture and went on wetting his house. Matt shrugged. The fire department could do a lot of things, but it could not rope adults like cows at a rodeo and remove them from their own personal rooftops.

What he really could not understand were the crowds. Tourists from the neighborhood. Tourists from the other side of LA. Disneyland let's-do-a-fire-instead tourists.

He would have thought the heat would drive them away. It was ninety degrees by itself, and with the fire approaching it felt like a hundred and ten. Or even a hundred and fifty. But there they stood, bare armed, bare legged, dripping sweat, and the smoke collecting in their sweat so that they turned muddy, and they didn't care. It was very windy. Combine Santa Ana winds with the fire's own weather and you had a gale. People just laughed and took pictures of each other with the fire as backdrop. Whoever sold disposable cameras was having a great day.

It was sort of like a party, with fire gossip instead of divorce gossip. "Laguna Beach has lost over three hundred homes," said somebody, gloating because she didn't live in Laguna Beach.

"Altadena's even worse," said somebody, bragging because she did live in Altadena, but in a paved citified area where it was unlikely the fire would reach.

June had been on the handy-talkie. Matt loved those; he loved all the equipment that went with firefighting. "Which houses you assigning us?" asked Matt.

She shook her head, meaning it was up to her crew. "Choose winners," said June. "Get houses you can defend and set up on 'em."

Choose winners.

Matt Marsh's parents certainly did not think they had raised a winner. They had brought him up to be a winner, all right: a corporate leader or a fine attorney who also played tennis and sailed. What was this firefighter crap? It made them crazy. They'd given him a Maserati for his birthday, to entice him back into the world of large incomes. As a firefighter, however, Matt couldn't afford the kind of neighborhood where people drove hundred-thousand-dollar cars. He was in the kind of neighborhood where people ripped them off, and took the wallets and possibly the lives of their drivers. So the Maserati sat, a glittering high velocity reproach, in his parents' garage on Pinch Canyon.

Matt Marsh wanted to win. He wanted to make saves — a house or a garage, but preferably a life. He wanted to show his mother and father that he had worth. There was no greater act than to rescue another human being.

Because of the hundred-and-fifty- to two-hundred-foot-high flames along some parts of this fire, Command expected significant civilian and firefighter injury. Nice word, "significant." It meant "lots and lots."

A medical branch had been established: five

paramedic units and ten ambulances. Available hospital beds had been inventoried.

Matt thought of the danger, and hoped and hoped and hoped that he would be right there when it came.

the Press house
3:30 P.M.

Danna was thinking about when she babysat for Geoffrey. She didn't like it. He didn't sit in your lap when you read a picture book to him, he wouldn't answer when you chatted, and he didn't kiss back when you kissed him good night.

What sitting for Geoffrey really was, was heartbreaking. You kept thinking that *this* hug would change him. *This* tickle would make him giggle and *this* kiss would make him beam at you. But affection didn't make a dent in Geoffrey.

You couldn't even accuse Mr. and Mrs. Aszling of neglecting him, although they did. Geoffrey neglected right back. He didn't have a personality, and after a while you didn't think of him as a little boy, just a breathing thing up there in the house.

She glanced at her watch, and sure enough, the 3:30 where-are-the-children-and-are-they-using-their-time-well phone call came through.

"Hey, sweetie," said Daddy. "How was school? You have a good day? Started your homework yet?"

"It was okay. We had fire drills. Bo-ring. I'm hanging around doing vocabulary. Don't you think there should be legislation against vocabulary?"

Her father laughed. "What's Hall doing?"

"I think he's swimming laps."

"Tell him to do his chemistry."

"Daddy, he *knows* to do his chemistry. At some point, you have to let *us* decide when to do what."

"Tell your mother," he said, and they both laughed, and air-kissed and hung up. Danna forgot her father completely and instantly.

If there's a fire, thought Danna, Hall would save Geoffrey.

She loved the image of her older brother saving a life. Hall was a funny combination of jock (hill climbing, off road biking) and dreamer. It was nice to have a brother only a year older, to pave the way and make clear what mistakes, teachers, and people to avoid.

Hall saves Geoffrey, she decided, and I save the kittens and I'd better also save Egypt and Spice.

Egypt and Spice were the Luus' horses. Every day Danna saved her school cafeteria apple, walking on up to the paddock to give Egypt one half and Spice the other.

She got an apple ready, and a laundry basket

for the kittens, and paused briefly to take in the news.

News never seemed possible to Danna, especially LA news. No matter how awful LA was made to look on network news, for people like Danna, who actually lived here, LA remained flawless. Killings, gangs, fires, riots, unemployment — they weren't *her* LA. Her LA was sunny comfort, hot colors, and cool drinks.

Danna had been to New York City a couple of times and could not believe people lived like that. Dirty and cold and grim. Crowded and mean under a gray sky and without flowers. And they were so superior about it, too. As if LA were nothing but a herd of automobiles and airheads gone amuck.

Indeed, on television, the Pacific Coast Highway was crowded with fire-fleeing automobiles — overflowing with possessions and people, even horses tied to bumpers, which Danna would certainly never do with any horse. The cars themselves were jousting with official rescue vehicles (and winning, because the trucks were following the rules and the cars weren't) — indeed, LA was nothing this afternoon but automobiles gone amuck. Danna switched the nonsense off. Okay, now what about stuff? she said to herself. Everything in my bedroom?

Should she rescue her Nancy Drew books? (Of course she was much too old to read them now, but went on buying them to complete her collection.) Her mother's girlhood collection of

Cherry Ames, Student Nurse books? (Danna had never read them, since the mere thought of hanging around sick people made her sick, too; Mom said that Cherry Ames hardly ever spent any time with sick people either, since she was far too busy solving mysteries and meeting handsome men.) Her pink sneaker collection? (Mom had bought Danna pink sneakers since size newborn, and Danna had saved them all. She had dozens.)

Then it occurred to Danna that she and Hall had no car. Mom had hers, Dad had his, and the garage was empty. So the matter of pink sneakers and nurse novels was solved.

We'd ride Egypt and Spice out, she thought. She envisioned herself with kittens in her arms, holding the reins, while Geoffrey sat in Hall's lap and they galloped over fire and flame.

What a film.

She would have to remember the camcorder. It would be great footage.

the brushfire
3:35 *P.M.*

A little bitty fire, like a campfire you built in the wrong place, you just buried with dirt, killing the oxygen. For a bigger fire — a dead tree burning — you needed a chain saw to cut the tree down and then the shovel to dig up some dirt and bury your tree in a pit. A fire that was above you, moving from treetop to treetop, gave you time to make your moves and calculate what to do next.

But a fire that belongs to the wind, or makes the wind — that fire moves as fast as the wind, because it *is* the wind.

Your ax, your chain saw, your shovel — they don't stop a fire whirl any more than a teaspoon empties a swimming pool.

The firefighters east of Grass Canyon stood where the fire no longer was. Orange flames left them behind at an incredible rate of speed. The earth under their feet after-smoked, the way when an earthquake is over, it after-shocks.

The fire did not burn toward Grass Canyon Road, where there were crews and equipment waiting for it, but into the wildness that lay so astonishingly close to such a huge metropolis.

The crew stumbled toward their truck to get on a radio and let Command know what had just happened: An ordinary fire had just become lethal.

But everybody in Los Angeles was on a frequency at that moment. Fire engines and ambulances from fifty towns, either under threat themselves, or volunteering to help their neighbors, sheriffs and the Red Cross and volunteers and commuters in their thousands and thousands of cars, highway patrol and paramedics, news stations and auxiliaries and command posts . . . radios, pagers, cellular, and hard-wired telephones were overloaded.

This transmission did not go through.

the Severyn house
3:38 P.M.

When Beau drove off, Elisabeth ran down the switchbacks of their steep driveway to hide from him.

Elisabeth, unlike Beau, could not care less about their house. It was a great big sterile place. You could houseclean inside with a garden hose; it was no different from the pools and the atrium. What Elisabeth loved was the bottom of the driveway.

There, where the oaks curled up in huge dark fists and the ferns grew as high as her waist, fallen rocks from some ancient mudslide formed a triangular hidey hole. It was too dark to read there, and Elisabeth was a reader, books by the armload, so she didn't stay long when she visited, but it was hers, and she went there most days for a minute or two. In the hidey hole she was safe.

Safe from her parents' disapproval.

Safe from remembering that she was never going to have flaxen hair and blue eyes and a winning smile.

Her mother did not know what to think of Elisabeth's reading. When Mom caught Elisabeth with a book, she said Elisabeth had no life; she was substituting books for a real life. Mom might even say that Elisabeth had no friends and was trying to turn paper and print into a friend. Elisabeth did not have friends, and it was terrible, and the only thing more terrible was her own mother accusing her of it.

If Beau was home, it would be okay, because Mom adored Beau, who was well named. Beau would distract Mom, and Elisabeth could slip away. But when Elisabeth was alone with Beau, it was bad in another way. Beau had decided that he was his sister's Only Hope. He would tutor and train and teach and coax and bribe until she was up to standard.

Some other time, Beau, she thought, ducking into the ferns.

The air was awful. She hated these dumb brushfires; it hurt to breathe. It turned the sky ugly and left a litter of ash on the swimming pool surface.

She had a pack of Sno Balls, her favorite junk food: cupcakes whose thick rubbery pink icing could be peeled off in one piece and stand on its own, like an igloo, while Elisabeth ate the inside.

Beau didn't know about the hidey hole. He was not the type who crept around hiding in woodsy thickets. He was the type who sought, or who was given, limelight. What did limelight mean, anyway? Why not lemonlight, or orange-light?

It was very dark in Elisabeth's hidey hole. And even though she was annoyed with the fires for giving her a cough, she was not thinking about fires. Brushfire sounded to an eight-year-old like something you would brush away, something on the floor you'd sweep up with a broom. Who would be afraid of that?

If the world did turn orange and lemon, Elisabeth Severyn would not know until it was too late.

the brushfire
3:38 P.M.

The fire sucked in oxygen. It turned into a white and yellow avalanche, shrieking both up and down the sides of hills, eating not just grass and not just brush, but anything living or lifeless in its path: eating paint off cars and melting handles off doors and burning antlers off deer.

It was traveling at the incredible speed of twenty miles an hour. Unless stopped, slowed, or blown backward, the safety zone between the inferno and Pinch Canyon would last only fifteen minutes.

ABSOLUTELY NO SMOKING

the gatehouse
3:38 P.M.

The afternoon grew hotter.

The houses on Pinch Canyon and Grass Canyon preheated like ovens, growing closer and closer to the temperature that would make them explode.

The air-conditioning in the tiny gatehouse failed. Alan Davey sat gasping for breath. He had to wear a uniform, because they liked uniforms on their help, these rich Pinch Canyon people; it made them feel pampered and special.

Alan Davey hated his job. He had meant to work in fine restaurants and become a television chef, but he'd failed. Failure was fine in California as long as it was a step to success. But Alan Davey was no chef. Short-order cook, maybe — fried eggs and pancakes — but not great food. The California dream had not come true for Alan Davey, and he was too tired and hostile to try again.

Being a residential guard should have been momentary, until he got on his feet again, but Alan Davey never found his feet again. Whereas everybody on Pinch — young, middle-aged, and old — had never been *off* their feet. He especially resented the teenagers, so casually sure of themselves, driving cars that cost more than Alan Davey would earn in years.

Beau. It might be pronounced Bo, but it was short for beautiful. That's what lived on Pinch Canyon. The beautiful people. And Alan Davey's life was so low now that he had to smile, and remember names, and leap to open the gates for a spoiled brat named Beautiful.

He wouldn't mind at all if these people lost everything.

Not that it would happen to them. They would laugh — fine white teeth surrounded by perfect golden tans — and rebuild bigger and better in the exact same place, because nothing on earth did affect them in the end. The guard wanted something to affect them.

When the air-conditioning failed, he thought, That's it. I quit. They're on their own. Who needs this?

He got his car (hidden behind pines so its age and lack of style would not offend Pinch Canyon owners) and abandoned his post. As a final thumbing of the nose, he locked the gate. These people specialized in being helpless; they loved being rich enough to pay somebody to do absolutely everything for them.

So there. No little rectangle of plastic would open that gate now. Let them sit there and fume and be helpless for a while.

Pacific Coast Highway
3:38 P.M.

"Hey, Pop," said Swann, "look over there."

Her father had worried about driving in California. They were supposed to have these ten-lane highways where you had to fight the heaviest traffic in the world. But it turned out that the heaviest traffic in the world was also pretty much the slowest.

The Gormans had come for Disneyland, and also, of course, the Universal Studios tour and Beverly Hills High and the boardwalks at Venice Beach and Knott's Berry Farm, if they had time. Frankly, they were a little annoyed. California weird was not coming through. People looked pretty darn normal. Mr. Gorman felt like he should get some money back.

And it wasn't relaxing like it was supposed to be. Everybody was distracted by these stupid wildfires, and the air stank. The green lawns everybody watered were a sort of creepy emerald, like fake contact lenses, while everyplace else was as dry and crispy as potato chips. The stupid wind never stopped, and you could never get enough to drink; your throat was always dried out.

"Oh, wow!" cried Swann, waving and pointing across the road and up into the hills. "Fires! Aren't they neat? Look at them all. I thought it would come in a sheet, but it's more like pockmarks."

"That one is a whole house," said Swann's mother eagerly. "Lookit, lookit, over there, it's a television van! Reporters! Let's follow them."

"Yeah, Pop," said Swann, "let's watch stuff burn."

Mr. Gorman followed the network van off the next exit and they began working their way in the direction of smoke and sirens. LA was dusty tan and rapidly turning gray in the smoke, but the fires were orange and scarlet and ruby. So bright!

There were two lines of traffic: the people running away from fire, loaded down by kids and pets and boxes, and then the people going toward the fires, to check them out and get some action, maybe see a house burn, maybe even with a person in it. Somebody was trying to direct traffic away from the fires instead of toward them, but the TV van ignored that, so the Gormans did, too.

They leaped out of their car only fifty feet away from a real house fire! This was what they'd flown all this way to see! This was great. Fire leaped out like bright-colored flowers. The houses had to be four or five times larger than any house back home. Every single house had at least a three-car garage.

"Wood shingle roofs," said her father in disgust. "These people are nuts. Who would live in a place where every time you turn around you got fire and earthquake and riots and queers and all kindsa people don't speak English." He shook his head. "Just to get a tan," he said. "People that dumb, they deserve to have their houses burn down."

Wow, you could heat Campbell's soup on the sidewalk, it was so hot.

Swann looked for the television van, because she was wearing a really nice pair of shorts.

On the wooden roof, a guy stood like he was standing on his patio, hosing down his roof, his bottle of beer in his other hand. "Man after my own heart," said Mr. Gorman.

The guy's hedge burst into flames, and the firefighters aimed their hose at it and the fire went out right away. Swann was kind of disappointed. She had hoped the guy's house would catch fire while he was trapped up there. That would have been exciting. Of course, you never said that kind of thing out loud, even though you knew every other person here was hoping for it too, and so instead they applauded the firefighters.

"Hey," said one firefighter, neon yellow jacket dripping with soot-blackened water. "Hey, don't go past the trucks. You people go on home, huh? This isn't a sideshow."

"Whole city's a sideshow," said Swann's father, and the fire tourists laughed.

the brushfire
3:42 *P.M.*

Hidden by smoke as dense as wool blankets, the fire crossed a minor unnamed hill, and dipped into a minor unnamed gully. These were not worth naming on maps, but they were road enough for a fire. Down in the reaches and gullies was a carpet of sagebrush, sumac, and scrub oak. Every leaf crackled like a dead thing, and every blade of grass was brown and sere.

The fire had miles of uninhabited acres to play with, where it could leap across bare spots and jump feet first into the fuel. It didn't need roads. It could make its own highway.

Ahead of the fire ran anything with legs: every wild and desperate creature trying to find sanctuary.

Pacific Coast Highway
3:43 *P.M.*

Mr. and Mrs. Aszling loved the word *everyone. Everyone* is writing a script, they were always saying. *Everyone* is trading up for a better house. *Everyone* is in mutual funds now.

Not everyone, thought Chiffon. Out of jealousy, she took Mrs. Aszling's best sunglasses and some of Mr. Aszling's spare dollars as well as the car keys.

Chiffon had lied about her age to get the job. She knew the Aszlings knew, and even so, they didn't care. Geoffrey didn't matter that much to them. Chiffon was not quite eighteen, having skipped her senior year in high school in order to become a star in Hollywood. You had to do something while you were waiting to be cast, but one day of waitressing proved to Chiffon that she was no waitress. In Chiffon's opinion, people should get their own silverware. So she took up child care.

She and Geoffrey were a good fit. She didn't pay any attention to him and he didn't pay any attention to her. The Aszlings were never home. Chiffon didn't think you could call it a home when you spent so little time there, but their absence had plusses. Whirlpool, sauna, media room, wet bar, and most of all, cars, might as well be hers.

As for the little girl from Peru or Belize or wherever, Elony was a silent, smoking presence, always listening to her dumb radio station and eating her smelly food. Elony had one plus. She was there and nobody could accuse Chiffon of leaving Geoffrey alone.

Chiffon had bailed out to go enjoy the fires. They weren't going to get any action on Pinch Canyon, and Chiffon wanted to see stuff burning from up close. She didn't like mountain roads. Who wanted a view of LA from high up? All you saw was this immense flat platter of housing — twenty million people, and not one cared what

Chiffon did next. Well, she didn't care what they did either, so there.

Chiffon whipped out Pinch, down Grass, and toward the Pacific Coast Highway. That was such a cool road. Pacific Ocean blue and glittering on your one side, and leaping high hills and houses skidding off them during mud slides on your other side. But there was too much traffic and no fire. She swung a U-ie and headed back up Grass Canyon, following smoke like a hunting dog.

The first fire she came upon, heading northeast on Grass Canyon Road, was small and cozy. It reminded Chiffon of camping: a cute little fire, all tucked into the stones, eager to toast a few marshmallows.

Cute guys, with their face masks off and their bandannas on, were shoveling at the edge of fires. You'd think they were making beds, they were so relaxed. They shoveled a little dirt, hacked at a few shrubs, laughed, sipped from canteens. The fire was around their knees and sometimes they'd even stick their shovels right into it, and not act like there was any danger at all. It was obvious that everybody was having a great time.

It must be a working requirement for firemen to be cute. Chiffon checked them out carefully. Of course, she was going to marry a producer, an agent, or a scriptwriter. But a fireman would be cute and muscular and for now, who cared about anything else?

This was a great spot. It was really busy here. Long trailer vans from the sheriff's department, fire department, and hospitals were surrounded by smaller vehicles like ducklings around their mother. There seemed to be a hundred fire engines, from all kinds of towns. There were hundreds of evacuated residents and their cars, repair trucks from the utility companies and phone company, television crews interviewing anybody, and snack trucks trying to make a dollar selling tacos or hot dogs.

Chiffon bought a Coke through the car window and spotted a really cute one.

She annoyed all the Mercedes, Land Rovers, and Volvos by cutting through them and parking right there. In traffic. She was pretty sure the really cute fireman would ask her to move the Corvette. If she couldn't get a date out of that, her name wasn't Chiffon.

the Aszling house
3:44 P.M.

Elony sighed and trudged back up the hill to be with the baby. You'll get your reward in heaven, she told herself.

But who wanted rewards in heaven? Elony was already half Californian. She wanted her reward right now.

She managed to smile at that, had another cigarette, and then went in to check on Geoffrey. Both of them loved popcorn. Maybe she'd pop some corn and lie on the rug with him and see if she could coax him to change channels. He clung to the remote like a pacifier so as to remain in control of the television, at least.

The outside light was reflecting annoyingly on the TV screen when she joined Geoffrey. She yanked the drapes shut so they wouldn't have to look at that spooky wine-glow sky, sat down beside him, and combed his hair for a while. Geoffrey loved to have his hair combed. Chiffon didn't know that. His parents didn't know. Only Elony knew.

Geoffrey refused to surrender the remote control and Elony didn't wrestle with him, but drifted into a nap.

the Severyn house
3:45 P.M.

The air settled like grease and Beau's white shirt began to turn gray. He couldn't find Elisabeth and he couldn't settle down. He was having some weird primitive response to distant smoke. If he were in touch with nature, he would know what it was saying to him. But he knew nothing. He could only pace, and feel anxious, and avoid the living room with the box on the mantel.

Beau circled from one deck to another, peering toward the dead end of Pinch Canyon. Usually he liked how he sort of had his own personal continent here: his hills on three sides and his own road to the ocean. Today . . .

Where's Elisabeth? he thought irritably. "Lizzie!" he shouted. His anxiety became a queasy pre-flu feeling in his gut.

In the last few months — since the box, as a matter of fact — Beau had become ridiculously protective of his little sister. What if Mom and Dad turned on Elisabeth, the way Dad had turned on Michael? After all, she wasn't up to standard either.

Elisabeth and Beau's father had been married before. Dad was much older than Mom. Mom was his trophy wife. Everybody laughed about this (except, presumably, the first wife). Beau wouldn't know, because he had never met the first Mrs. Severyn. There had been a son by this marriage: Michael. Beau had had a half brother. They had never met either. Dad's divorce had been so ugly that there was total separation between the first and second families.

Michael died.

AIDS.

Dad had been sent the box of ashes that had once been Michael. It was all that existed of Michael now. Literally. When Dad had found out that Michael was gay, years ago, he'd destroyed every photograph, every old report card, art project, and outgrown baseball uniform. He had never seen that son again.

Dad had set the box of his son's ashes on the mantel, as if planning to do something momentarily, but it had been there for months. Dad could neither bury the box nor move it.

Mom said nothing about it, and as for Michael's mother, Beau did not even know her name, nor why she hadn't kept the ashes herself, or even if she was alive.

Throughout his teens, Beau had been aware of his father watching for "signs" that this son, too, might be gay. Beau knew perfectly well he was not, and yet to tell his father this, to give him peace of mind on the subject, would in some way betray Michael.

Sometimes Beau conversed with this dead brother he knew only by box. So Michael, were you a nice guy or what? Would you have spoken to me if your mom and our dad hadn't hated each other? Would you and I have been real brothers, maybe even friends, if my mom hadn't ruined your mom's marriage?

"Elisabeth!" called Beau one more time.

The sky changed dramatically. One minute it had been wine red, with layers of pink and gold and yellow, and now it was blackening. Wow, thought Beau. That's great. We're going to have rain. That'll help the fires.

He coughed. The air was so hot. It was burning

his throat to breathe. He ought to stay in the air-conditioning. But when he was in a mood like this, Beau hated to be alone in the house with those ashes. Those betrayed, unloved, unwanted parts of Michael.

Beau knew a cheerleader who lived the opposite side of this story. Katie was the first-time-around child, and her father never so much as remembered her birthday. But the two little babies of his second marriage, he loved lavishly, spending time and money and energy and adoration on his second family.

Beau didn't think there were explanations for men who did that. If Beau cornered him and said, Dad, are you going to abandon us some day too?, Dad would be astonished. Dad would say, What are you talking about? Beau would say, Michael, I'm talking about Michael. And Dad would glare at him for mentioning the forbidden name and shout, What does he have to do with anything?

What does he have to do with anything? thought Beau. Get a grip on yourself.

His parents despised people who lacked self-discipline. So the thing was to discipline Michael out of his thoughts.

The thundercloud gathered itself strangely behind the bulk of Pinch Mountain. It looked as if a prairie tornado was snaking around back there, half hidden by the hills. Do we have tornadoes in California? thought Beau. We have everything else.

the Severyn house
3:46 *P.M.*

In her hidey hole, Elisabeth thought about the ghost.

Ghosts belonged in East Coast sea captains' houses, where spirits of murdered brides could not rest. A ghost in the bright laughing sun of southern California? Dumb casting.

But Los Angeles had a ghost. Not on Pinch Canyon, for which she was very thankful. But pretty close. Next door to the riding stable she went to.

It hadn't been that bad of a fire, only eight houses, and they saved the barn. The man had gotten safely out of his house. He was not burned. He was not overcome by smoke. He was among fire trucks and firefighters, protected by fat hoses spraying blessed water.

And then he ran back into the burning house, shouting that he had to get something.

He never came out.

He had lived alone, that man. There were no people inside who needed to be rescued. He had no pets. No cocker spaniel, no beloved cats to save. So what had he needed so much? What could it have been? Photographs? Silver? A souvenir from some old vacation?

Nobody ever knew.

They knew only that it was more important than life. That man had chosen to die in the most awful way there was. He had not died by breathing in the smoke first. He had died by burning up.

Some well-to-do couple purchased the property without a shudder and rebuilt the house, making it finer, wider, and broader. Elisabeth knew he was in there still, that ghost. Cold and shadowy, still reaching for whatever it was he could not live without. She half-saw him every time she went riding at the stable, his fingers burning black before they could rescue the sacred object.

There was nothing in Elisabeth's house she could not live without. Tucked under the deep glossy leaves, crouched in hot shadow, Elisabeth let her real worry form.

What would her parents rescue, if their house burned? Would they put Elisabeth first? They never had.

Elisabeth saw little of her mother or father even when they weren't at work. They were both very concerned with their bodies, and belonged to an important and prestigious health club. Their fitness regimes took a great deal of time, and Mom's class where she worked on her inner child could never be skipped.

It was pretty easy to skip the real children, however.

Elisabeth ate both cupcakes. She wanted to belong to a family where they had purple and yellow and aqua colored sugar cereal around. When she grew up, fresh fruit would never cross her threshold, and as for foreign vegetables, she would pay the supermarket not to carry them. She would eat Twinkies and Sno Balls and lots and lots of salty greasy potato chips.

Overweight made Mom tremble. She liked best the people who stopped eating after one bite of dessert and sat quietly through the rest of the conversation without ever touching that chocolate again. These people had discipline.

Elisabeth didn't want discipline. She wanted a pet. Specifically, one of Danna Press's kittens. She'd asked her mother, but as far as Elisabeth's mother was concerned, pets were just hair on your couch and fleas on your ankles.

Elisabeth Severyn slid into a nightmare where her parents rescued the things that count, and she was not one.

A deer joined her in the thicket and woke her from the dream.

It was scary and spooky and perfect.

The deer was small and blond. Its eyes were immense. Its flanks heaved. Elisabeth sat entirely still. She could not believe her good fortune.

Perhaps my real skill will be with wild animals, she thought. Perhaps I'll make great films in Africa, or soothe gentle beasts, or learn how dolphins talk.

The deer saw her and was not afraid.

Ohhhhhh, thought Elisabeth, loving the deer.

It did not occur to Elisabeth that the deer had far greater things to be afraid of.

the Press house
3:46 P.M.

Hall paddled occasionally, getting new angles on Pinch Mountain. Its fuzzy watercolory look never changed. Hall never saw an animal on the mountainside. He always looked, thinking that surely a deer or coyote must appear. But they never did. Of course, maybe from here, what, a half mile away, or something, they blended invisibly.

Today was different.

Somebody had thrown a basketball up there. Or something orange. Hall couldn't imagine how they'd done it. Or from where.

The swimming pool was practically boiling. Plus he was turning pruny from being in the water for so long. If he had to run from a fire right now, he'd be so waterlogged it wouldn't even singe his eyebrows. This was not turning out to be a restful afternoon. The whole world was hotting up. California was letting him down.

Letting him down. He was always hearing that phrase. Just the other night, Dad had used it about Matt Marsh.

Matt Marsh had been one of the spectaculars: good in sports and school, popular with kids and parents, clever at technology and music, and, of course, handsome and cool. And what happened? After a few semesters in college, Matt dropped out for a job in one of the more boring suburbs down in the Valley — a flat omelette of a place where people with personality didn't go, and if they went, after a few months they had no personality left.

Matt Marsh not only moved to this pathetic part of LA, he became a firefighter, washing his little truck, folding his little hose, memorizing his little manual. Once you were a firefighter, that was what you were: a firefighter. You couldn't rise like a meteor to splendid success on another level, become a vice president or a producer.

It was okay to do clerical work before the casting session that would make you a star. It was okay to bus dishes between auditions. But it was not okay to choose something forever that went no place.

Matt Marsh, of all people. Nobody even talked about him anymore. He might as well have been dead, and his parents were embarrassed.

"They gave that kid everything," Hall's father had said sadly just the other night, "and look at how he turned out."

It was scary, hearing about guys that let their fathers down. Hall was desperately afraid of not pleasing his father. How was he supposed to tell Dad he wanted to help little guys like Geoffrey turn into people? "Maybe Matt'll save lives," Hall had pointed out.

"If you or Danna did something like that, I'd be frantic," said Mom bluntly. "I expect great things of you."

So it was not just Dad. It was Mom, too, expecting great things of Hall.

Hall swam one slow-motion lap, floated on his back, and in rolling over caught a glimpse of the rusty orange basketball again.

It was larger.

More orange.

the health club
3:46 P.M.

Beau and Elisabeth's mother was on the treadmill. Her two best friends were on treadmills on either side of her, Joy listening to a motivational tape and Suze telling how her ex-husband number two was now ending his marriage number three and should Suze begin dating him again?

This was far more interesting than the problem Wendy Severyn had: her daughter. Thinking about Beau was delightful. Thinking about Elisabeth was depressing.

You were supposed to accept your children as they were, but when the child was Elisabeth, hiding out in thickets or reading at the back of closets instead of giggling with other little girls . . . oh, why couldn't Elisabeth have a real life? Wendy Severyn resolved to invite a new child over every day, one after another, no matter how much her daughter or the guest whined

about it. There had to be *someone* who'd want
to be friends with Elisabeth.

"The fires are spreading," said Joy suddenly.

"You're listening to the radio?" said Wendy.
"I thought you had a tape on."

"The fires fascinate me. I can't get enough of
them. The power of nature is still here, no matter how we try to put a lid on it. The awesome
strength," said Joy reverently, "of untamed nature."

Wendy Severyn hated nature. Nature meant
bodies that got old, and Wendy intended to beat
nature and keep her body young.

"Wendy," said Joy, "it just hit Grass Canyon."

Grass Canyon was a very long road. The fire
was not necessarily anyplace near Pinch Canyon. Anyway, Aden had said not to worry.
Wendy had enough to worry about, what with
turning Elisabeth into a child she could be proud
of.

Suze acted as if the fire was already in Pinch
Canyon, for heaven's sake. "Your driveway is
awfully narrow, Wendy," said Suze. "And those
switchbacks? You couldn't even use a regular
moving van, remember? I doubt if firetrucks can
make the corners either."

The treadmill kept moving. You could not
stop your pace because the ground beneath you
did not stop its pace. So Wendy went on running
and running and running. "Beau is a sensible
boy," she said. "I'm sure he'll know what to do.
If only Elisabeth were a sensible girl."

"Poor you," Suze commiserated. Suze's two daughters were lovely little copies of Suze, which was so unfair. By rights, Elisabeth should have been a copy of Wendy.

Wendy turned the dial to make the treadmill go faster. If she were really running, she wouldn't be able to think about anything at all, and wasn't that what meditation was all about? Emptying your mind?

Wendy Severyn did not know that even Beau, who loved his mother, believed she had a head-start on an empty mind.

the fire
3:57 P.M.

For fires, there is a verb that you use differently.

Flower.

A little fire can "flower" like a rose opening to the sun. It spreads, and its petals cover the ground. It tosses bouquets to the bottom canyon layer of sumac and brush, and that "flowers," too, and all around, more places "flower" until you are in a garden of wildfire, instead of a garden of wildflowers.

Some fires not only flower, they throw. They pick up burning logs and toss them ahead. These are fire whirls, giant smoke rings with a downdraft of deadly gases. Their center temperature can actually reach two thousand degrees.

In the dips and gullies and hills beyond Pinch Mountain, the fire played all its games. Here it slowed, and there it died. Here it leaped a huge space and there it pivoted and went back where it had been.

The wind blew into the fire's waiting mouth. The hotter the fire, the more oxygen it ate, the quicker the wind refilled the supply, and the hotter the fire became.

Behind Pinch Mountain was a narrow crevasse. Not a canyon, really, because it didn't open onto anything, just a slot in the earth. The fire fell down into it and the crevasse "blew" — a bomb exploding behind Pinch.

Los Angeles
3:57 *P.M.*

Hall and Danna's mother and father worked in the same studio. The studio was its own world, with deadlines and demands, absolutes and restrictions, hopes and fears. Like a hospital ward, it completely enclosed its people from other worlds. They forgot everything, swamped in the task at hand.

Oddly, here in a world utterly ruled by television, no television was on.

Mrs. Press had a watch that did everything

but write the scripts for her. Its alarm went off at regular intervals so she could be in touch with the children. Otherwise she'd forget them. It wasn't a matter of forgetting to call — she literally forgot they existed.

Sometimes when she was really immersed in a script, the people who lived on the page canceled out the people who lived in her house, and she would actually find herself wondering who Hall was, or who Danna was, and why. She believed that her children did not know this.

Over and over, Mrs. Press told herself that the kids were fourteen and fifteen now, they were responsible, they were good, they knew the rules . . . but today she worried. It was unusual for Jill Press to worry. She had brought up these children solidly; they did not wander from the yard and they did not wander from her rules.

This afternoon, there was a nag at the bottom of her heart, a constant low-level anxiety that she was doing something wrong. But her husband had just called. It was absurd to be calling again.

Absurd or not, Jill Press took her cellular phone and went to another room to call. (Danna got very cross if her parents talked to her in front of people, although Hall never noticed these things.)

She wished she could be home, teasing the kids, going horseback riding with them, peeling Hall away from that creepy little Aszling kid.

She thought of dinner, which once again the

four Presses were not going to have together.
Danna would have Frosted Flakes followed by
several ice cream sandwiches. Hall, so mature
in most ways, was a toddler for food: He'd mix
Sugar Smacks, BerryBerry Kix, and Cocoa Kris-
pies. Mrs. Press had met families who claimed
the children loved sprout sandwiches and tofu
casseroles but her children, personally, were
into sugar.

Once out of the conference room, she felt fool-
ish. Fourteen and fifteen was not four and five.
She couldn't have better kids. What was her
problem here? Did she think they were going to
go out and get hooked on cocaine this afternoon?
She was just itchy from too many meetings. It
was affecting her like a rash, that and the fires
and the Santa Ana winds.

She went back into the meeting and was re-
lieved that she hadn't bothered the children only
minutes after the last check-in.

Los Angeles
3:57 P.M.

Elisabeth and Beau's father also sat in a meeting. There were seven men and four women at
this meeting and he was annoyed at every one
of them. Why must they talk so much? In the
case of some of these people, why talk at all?

There were people in this world who should not have been provided with mouths.

He was sitting between two of them.

The talk was of the fires, but only what the fires were doing to network advertising income. Fire raged in a dozen places: Glendale and Laguna Beach and Pasadena and Ventura. Nobody knew how any fire had started: lightning, cigarettes, arson, sparks from dragging broken mufflers of passing cars. Now, in the high wind, with the land and the scrub preheated, fire seemed to be starting itself.

In this group, nobody cared how the fires started. They had bigger things to worry about. Car dealers, for example, didn't like to advertise during broadcasts of fires that were consuming their customers.

Mr. Severyn glanced at his watch. This meeting could last until six or even seven. He was not a homebody. Getting home in time for dinner was not something that normally ran through his mind, but these fires were getting on everybody's nerves. They'd gone on too long and there were too many of them.

Pinch Canyon was safe. The neighborhood association paid a security guard and if something happened . . .

But he felt a queer pounding in his chest. A sort of primitive awareness. It was not like Beau to phone him at work. Beau knew that was reserved for emergencies.

In the complete lack of privacy at this hostile

meeting, Aden Severyn allowed himself some very private thoughts. He was angry at himself for the whole nonsense over Michael's ashes. He did not believe in a life after death, and he certainly did not believe that Michael inhabited those ashes sitting in that cardboard box on the mantel.

He'd seen Beau's eyes flicker toward the box every time he went through the room, seen his son flinch just thinking about them.

He'd seen Elisabeth design a detour for herself so she didn't have to pass the fireplace. The whole family had moved its activities to the far side of the house, as if they really did intend to bury Michael up there, and would always skirt the graveyard.

He had to talk to Beau. And for that matter, to Michael himself. It was strange how death had brought Michael into his mind as life never had.

Mr. Severyn's chest actually hurt. The possibilities were: heart attack (in the advertising industry, people had heart attacks quite regularly); indigestion (considering what he had had for lunch, this was very possible); and panic.

Those fires are miles away from the house, he told himself.

He heard his own thought: not *miles away from the children*, but *miles away from the house*.

A creepy damp wash, like a muggy day, slid up his entire body, enveloping him in what was either a stroke or a warning of one. He said, "I can't sit here. The fires worry me. I'm going home to be there with the kids." He liked that sentence.

"You can't get there from here," said the woman who should have been born without a mouth. "The highway is closed."

The highway was closed? What was she talking about?

"People are being evacuated," she said, "and the traffic has blocked the highways. You can't get home."

You can't get home. It had certainly been true for Michael.

Aden Severyn wanted no parallels, no lessons. *"What? Why didn't you tell me?"* He was shouting, planning the woman's strangulation.

"You never want to hear anything I have to say," she said triumphantly.

the Press house
3:59 P.M.

Hall was out of the pool, wandering mindlessly, postponing the homework. The orange basketball expanded.

Below it, five cyclists in neon bright lycra suits appeared on the narrow path that wound around Pinch Mountain. A few years ago there had been no such path, but dirt bikers loved

Pinch, and had worn a path into the sides. When there were mud slides the path had to be restarted, but that was just a fun new challenge.

Hall was startled to realize how large the orange basketball was. Now that the cyclists were there for comparison, he saw that it was as big as a car. It was hanging over the bikes like a boulder soon to roll down. He could only suppose they didn't see it; that the levels of the mountain blocked their view. They stopped pedaling, and looked around, confused. They had goals. Plans. An itinerary, probably. Hall expected that they had backpacks, water bottles, sandwiches. They didn't see anything, but perhaps they heard something, or felt something.

Was it fire? But there weren't any flames. It had to be fire, and yet it had none of the traditional fire-type look. A huge coal, maybe? Where could it have come from? There was no bigger fire here. Had somebody started it? Had some arsonist crept up there with a match? But Hall had been out there, and checked the mountain as always, and as always it had been bare.

He stood in his bathing suit dripping on the tiles.

The orange mass widened.

The wind picked up. It was a hotter wind than usual, and because it was laden with grease and ash, he could *see* the wind. Watch the turbulence. The wind tied itself in knots and changed its mind about where to go.

Beyond the wind, the sky was a sunset on the

wrong side of the world. The sky turned magenta and gold and lemon and hot hot pink and vermilion.

"Dannie!" he shouted. "Danna, get the camcorder! We've got to film this. This is absolutely incredible footage. Dannie, come out here and look at this!"

Over the barren mountainside, above the bikers, came a herd of deer. They leaped over rocks and each other, crossing the path just below the cyclists, and rushing on down a mountainside too steep even for deer. They stumbled and fell on each other, scrambling desperately.

A huge solid black silhouette suddenly filled the sky. It was a smoke mountain. Or the top of an explosion.

Hall was awestruck. He could think of nothing else, look at nothing else. His sister joined him, holding the camera. It was palm-sized, light and easy to use, but she wasn't using it. she was as hypnotized as her brother.

It was fire, they knew that, but the fire itself wasn't there yet. This was its teaser. Its advance advertising.

Awesome, thought Halstead Press.

The smoke advanced past the mountain, as if the shadow of the mountain were going first instead of after. The smoke moved over the sphinx head that was Pinch and down the rocky gravelly side that became Pinch Canyon. The smoke was so much more colorful than Hall expected smoke to be: It was like an old bruise — black and gray and olive green. It had sound. It roared, a jet engine inside the mountain, a volcano bursting rock.

Like the deer, the bikers stumbled and fell on each other. Three whirled and pedaled wildly back the way they had come. The other two surged on.

Then, chasing its own smoke, came the fire.

Over the heads of the bicycle riders appeared a huge stretch of fire. It was brighter orange than the fruit. It was embroidered with splotches of crimson and gold, and its smoke was a universe of black before it and after it and in it.

For a few moments the fire was vertical, a sheet billowing on a giant's clothesline.

Neither Danna nor Hall could make a sound. They were stunned by the size of the sudden fire, the power of it, the absolute utter proof that it was fire, and not a joke.

The fire bent over like a predator and went after the bicycles.

RESIDENTS
ONLY

the Severyn house
4:00 P.M.

That it was a fire storm and not a rainstorm actually caught Beau by surprise. In spite of the dozen raging fires, in spite of the fact that he had been thinking of nothing but fire, he had not in fact expected fire. Not where *he* lived.

Fire stood on top of Pinch Mountain like grizzly bears rearing up to attack.

The fire seemed strangely stationary, as if it had found a good spot on the side of Pinch Mountain and planned to stage a program there. That was good, because obviously Beau had been wasting time wandering back and forth. He needed to be on the decks or the roof, wetting things down, preparing for the actual fight.

He couldn't do that unless he knew where Elisabeth was. What was the matter with her, choosing a time like this to go into hiding? Why did his sister have to be such a dumpling? "Elisabeth!"

He lifted the deck phone to see if she was talking to somebody on an extension, but the phone was — *the phone was out.*

He stared at the receiver. No dial tone, no response, nothing. It was just a plastic rectangle with buttons.

For Beau, whose life was built on wired or wireless communication, a nonworking phone was as frightening as fire. It paralyzed him, to realize he had no phone. The cordless phone, he thought, trying to pull together. Where's the cellular?

But he had no more idea where he'd set that down than where Elisabeth was. Besides, cellular was often less than useful in a canyon — microwaves didn't climb up and over the rock.

Beau could hear the fire.

Nobody had said that fire chewed. That you could hear its jaws cracking trees like a tiger's teeth cracking bones. Nobody had said that when fire split a tree in half, the tree *screamed*.

Crackling fire wasn't the sound of balling paper up in your fist. It sounded more like a freeway full of car accidents — metal and glass smashing.

His heart was pounding in a surprising way. You didn't think of your heart as a muscle until it pounded this hard, and then you knew it could get cramps and get exhausted just like your calves or thighs from running too hard.

He tried to guess how far away the fire was, in time and miles. It was roughly a half mile to the foot of Pinch Mountain, but up to the crest where the fire was, he couldn't seem to get his mind working in feet or yards. If I know where Elisabeth is, I'll be able to think clearly.

He ran to the pantry, an enormous storeroom

off the kitchen, and jerked open the empty bottom cabinet in which Elisabeth liked to play house. The cabinet door came off in his hand and it took Beau a moment to realize that he had actually ripped it off. Talk about adrenaline.

But adrenaline didn't matter. Finding Elisabeth did. He couldn't stand to have that fire out there, looming on top of Pinch Mountain like a beast with greedy fingers, and not know where his sister was. "Lizzie! Don't play games with me! Where are you?"

The house was utterly silent.

"Elisabeth! Fire! Pinch Mountain is on fire. You have to come out!" He checked her bedroom and bathroom, checked Mom's dressing room, where Elisabeth sometimes leafed through Mom's beautiful clothes, as if she wanted to play dress up and makeup, but didn't dare. He checked the computer room and the music room.

No Elisabeth.

He raced back to the deck to check the progress of the fire.

He had expected a slow, steady burning march, the way he had seen on television. But this fire was not marching. It had no front line. Instead it was throwing pieces of itself on ahead — embers, firecrackers, detonators. The canyon and the vertical yards and gardens were speckled with little fires. None was dangerous at this moment, but one strong wind and they would coalesce into a single fire, completely enveloping all twenty-one houses. For a moment he was paralyzed. Hideous evil sensation, straight out of nightmare. Stupid mind, stupid legs, stupid lungs.

"Elisabeth!" he bellowed. He felt a terrible anger with his sister for being in the wrong place when everything else was also wrong. He tried to stifle this. If she heard the anger in his voice, she would never come out.

At the circle on the end of Pinch Canyon Road, a homeowner had years ago planted a row of palms. A single palm tree crown had caught fire. The fire burned merrily at the top of the long thin trunk, like a match-lit brandy dish that a waiter was bringing to the table. It sat on the tray of the tree and burned quite prettily, nice colors, nice size.

All houses on Pinch were on the north side of the road. On the south, a single thread of fire, like an unrolling ribbon, was laying itself out on the narrow verge between pavement and canyon wall.

It could not accomplish much until it reached a wider place in the canyon.

The wider place was across from the Severyn driveway.

the Press house
4:01 P.M.

Danna was certainly glad that she had made kitten contingency plans. "You keep an eye on the fire, Hall," she said. "Wet the house with the garden hose. I'll get the kittens."

Danna chose the red plastic laundry basket that had fake basketweave through which the kittens could breathe. I'll cut cardboard to fit the top, she told herself, and tape it down so the kittens can't climb out. "Here, kitty, kitty, kitty," she called in a high soprano. One kitten came.

She rummaged around miscellaneous kitchen drawers hunting up scissors and tape. "Here, kitty, kitty, kitty." The laundry basket was bigger than she had expected and finding a lid was going to be a problem. The only cardboard box she turned up had once held a computer monitor. She'd poke breathing holes in the box and stuff the kittens in. But would seven kittens fit in such a small box? And why was she even bothering with the kittens?

She and Hall were not going to abandon the house, the house was far too important for that. Besides, it was pretty neat that Mom and Dad weren't here; she and Hall would have to rise to the occasion, and handle it themselves, and save everything.

She got out a can of stinky cat food and opened

it noisily. "Here, kitty, kitty, kitty. We don't have all day, you know."

But Danna thought that they did have all day. On television nobody seemed to be in that big of a rush. The fire was always at the edges of things, and never in the center of things, and it did not occur to Danna that this was because the cameraman did not want to get burned.

Danna had watched the fires on television for many hours over the last nine days, not to mention last year and the year before. The fire-fighting crews — men and women who flew in from various states as well as various towns — were equipped with shovels and a Pulaski — with which they attacked the edges of fires. They were very relaxed about it, as if the fire was nothing but a weed growing around their boots. They acted as if they really expected to kill the fire with a shovel of dirt here and a shovel of dirt there.

On television you saw people sitting on their decks and in their yards, watching the fires that threatened their homes. They might pack their cars just in case, but they stayed with the house, because somebody had to be there in case a wind carried a burning ember onto the roof and it had to be put out.

Danna discovered that six kittens strapped inside a cardboard box could scream as loud as varsity cheerleaders. "Sssshhhh," she told them. "People will think I'm torturing you." She carried the box, which bulged erratically as the kittens hurled themselves against their prison, into the front hallway just in case she really did have to take them somewhere. Then she decided to put a six pack of cold Cokes on top of the box just in case.

She assumed she would have as much time as she needed.

She had no sense that the fire was making the schedule, and they would have to stick to the fire's schedule or die.

the Severyn house
4:02 P.M.

Beau was up at the house, sounding like a madman, shrieking every possible variation on her name: *Elisabeth — Lizzie — Liz — Elisabeth Severyn!* If he didn't keep quiet, he'd scare the bunnies.

Elisabeth not only had deer in her hidey hole, but she had been joined by real bunnies, sitting at her feet. Little noses working like little engines, little floppy ears twisting and turning as if on strings that Elisabeth herself were pulling.

Elisabeth didn't answer Beau. Probably Mother or Daddy had phoned with instructions for how they were to spend the remainder of the day. Usefully. Elisabeth didn't want to spend her time usefully. She didn't want to improve her mind or her athletic or musical or social skills. She wanted to sit in the quiet green glade with suddenly tame rabbits and deer.

She held out her hand, but her guests didn't notice. They were panting, their little flanks heaving. "Come see me," she crooned. "Come let's be friends."

the fire
4:02 P.M.

Way above the stack of houses, a little bent tree clung to the canyon rim. It burned quietly. It didn't flame, it didn't turn orange and yellow, it didn't scream for attention.

The fire burned through its skinny little rock-squeezed trunk, and it became a five-foot torch. The smoke tornado threw the little tree downhill like a human sacrifice in some terrible ancient religion.

It tumbled against rock and gravel and dust, and came to rest on a ledge just below the Severyn house.

And there, on the underside of the deck, it prepared for human sacrifice.

Grass Canyon Road
4:03 P.M.

The house with the blazing roof was being abandoned. Swann could tell because the owner was sobbing as she scuttled in and out her front door with armloads of stuff that she threw into a magnificent car. Swann didn't even know what kind of car it was, but it was old, really old, museum old; and so was the woman. Elegant and thin, the way they were out here till they died, no gravy on biscuits for them. Her hair ought to be white but, of course, was still golden.

Swann put on her most understanding smile, her gentlest expression. She hurried over to the elderly woman. "May I help? I'd be happy to get this stuff packed better. You're wasting space. Here. I'll put this box on the floor and then we'll have more room on the seat. Quick, you go back and get some more."

"Oh, thank you!" said the woman, rushing away.

It was a jewelry box. Grinning, Swann carried her trophy back to her parents. Pop had already turned the car around. Swann and her family wisely moved on.

Of course the highway patrol kept trying to stop people from going north on Grass Canyon Road, and of course people kept ignoring them, because they wanted to be where the action was. It was cool. Cherokees and Blazers and Mercedes were streaming down toward the Pacific Coast

Highway. Some had not had time to get anything, and their shocked faces stared blindly out
of their car windows, as if they had forgotten
how to drive. People whose loss was so great
they really had forgotten how to drive stood on
the side of the road, sobbing.

"This is so neat," said Swann. She was pretty
sure the jewelry was real. "I'm glad we came to
California."

They stared for a while at a woman who
seemed to have been burned. Her clothing was
certainly charred, and her hands looked awfully
weird. She moved toward them, confused and
frightened, as if she needed help, so Swann's
father quickly accelerated around her.

Swann's mother put on the pearls that had
filled an entire drawer of the jewelry box, and
they laughed at the effect of those generous
strands against her obscene T-shirt.

A few blocks up, a firetruck barricaded the
road. Annoyed, they left their car and walked
past the barricades. The fires were very close
here and you could really watch houses burn. A
dozen houses into a cul-de-sac was a mansion
with an eight-car garage.

The firefighters were making a save, or trying
to, on the opposite side of the street. Mr. Eight
Cars was going crazy, trying to save them. "Garage has an asphalt roof, looks like vinyl siding,
definitely cement floors," said Swann's father.
"What's the guy worried about? That's not
gonna burn."

"If the fire gets hot enough, it'll melt them," pointed out Swann's mother.

They were pleased at the thought that these people would lose everything they owned.

the Press house
4:04 P.M.

Hall did not touch the garden hose. He stared at the distant path where the bicycles had been. There was no sign of them. Actually there was no sign of the path either, because smoke had taken over the mountain. Sometimes you could see flame and sometimes you couldn't. Hall couldn't figure out where the fire went when there was no flame.

It was even hotter. He had not thought the world could get this hot. He remembered hearing on television that the interior of a fire whirl could reach two thousand degrees. He tried to imagine what happened to riders of bikes in two-thousand-degree heat and then tried not to imagine it.

Were those cyclists just out for exercise, having forgotten that half the county was ablaze? Did they think it would be cool to get up close and personal to a fire wall? Or like Hall, had they counted on the fire to stay where it had been earlier in the day?

He was shivering. His feet felt pretty comfortable where they were. His stomach didn't feel so great where it was. His eyes burned, from ash and smoke and tears.

He was weeping for the cyclists.

They could not be alive.

Of course, they're alive, he said to himself.

He remembered nine-one-one. He had to phone. Let emergency people know that several people were hurt on Pinch Mountain. But you couldn't drive up Pinch in an ambulance. You couldn't land a helicopter on the vertical sides of it. You couldn't walk in, carrying stretchers and first aid kits, because there was fire between you and the bike path.

Hall's mind slowed down, like a bike coasting to a stop.

In the distance, a huge spinning ember of fire got caught in the whirlwind. The ember was as large as a bonfire, as large as a couch, and it spun as if it were only a feather. It landed in the driveway of the farthest-in house on the canyon: Matt Marsh's house.

The road sign read PINCH CYN. CYN never quite looked like the right abbreviation for Canyon. But you couldn't write CAN, either, as if you lived in a jar.

But we do live in a jar, thought Hall, *and the lid is about to close.*

"I've got all the kittens," said Danna. He was startled to have her next to him again. How long had he stood there accomplishing nothing?

"Now," said his sister, sounding exactly like

Mom. It was that list voice: chores, groceries, errands, orders. "We've got to get Egypt and Spice," said Danna. "Then we'll start defending the house."

The fire had two personalities. There was the sheet fire personality: a wall advancing down Pinch, still a considerable distance away. But closer were little fires, as if many careless campers were getting ready to make S'Mores.

Hall's hands were extremely cold. There was absolutely no sign on the mountain that there was, or ever had been, a row of bicycles. "I'm not sure we can defend the house," said Hall. They were on the grass — thick, lush, damp grass where sprinklers were going. Their legs and shoes were soaked while their hair and faces baked from the approaching fire. Usually the sprinklers ran at night. Hall wondered whether he had been the sensible person to turn the sprinklers on, and if so, what other actions he had taken.

"Of course we can," said Danna impatiently. "We've been watching people on TV all week stay with their houses."

The wall of fire was throwing baby fires out in front of itself, like an automatic baseball pitching machine.

"What a photo op!" said Danna.

The kittens were crazed by their enclosure. Their little claws and jaws attacked the cardboard and tape. It was a matter of seconds before Kumquat and Lemon ripped their way to freedom.

"We should call nine-one-one," said Hall.

A small plane flew over, and behind it, some distance away, a pair of helicopters. "They know, Hall," said Danna, with the exaggerated patience of sisters. "They'll be here in a minute. It's up to us to keep the roof wet and the horses safe until they arrive. Now. I'm bringing Egypt and Spice here."

Hall's head ached ferociously. A smoke ache. He wasn't pleased with how he was reacting to pressure. Dannie was full of plans. He didn't have any plans, just a sickening vision of horses and kittens on fire. No trace of them as there was no trace of the cyclists. Had those people burned to nothing? Was there just black ash where their hearts and lungs had been a minute ago? He tried to wet his lips, but the astonishing wind was like a clothes dryer, a tongue dryer.

The fire settled hungrily on the Marsh house. Usually you couldn't see the Marsh house from here, since it was the only house built on the true canyon bottom, and hidden by its trees. What you could see now, in fact, was not a house either — only the flames of its death. Mr. and Mrs. Marsh worked downtown. Their children were long grown up and gone, so there was no person there to worry about. Only the possessions of lifetimes.

"Dannie, I think maybe we'd better just leave."

"And abandon the house?" His sister was outraged. "What kind of wimp are you? Mom and

Dad wouldn't want us to do that. Anyway, you and I are going to get great footage. Where is that camera?"

What if I am a wimp? thought Halstead Press.

But whatever else might have been a wimp, the fire wasn't. It found a propane tank. The tank exploded like mortar fire. Blue-white flames shot vertically toward the rim of the canyon. The Marshes's house incinerated as Hall and Danna watched. It didn't simply burn. It and its trees were there and then they weren't there.

Wind bent the blue fire toward the next house. That had an orange tile roof, which wouldn't go quite so easily. But the yard, the gardens, the trees, and the sheds went in a finger snap.

Hall never thought of Pinch Canyon in horizontal terms. He didn't have a sense of how many houses were between him and the fire. When he thought of Pinch, he thought upward. Now he thought across. Only nine houses stood between the shared driveway and that inferno.

Shared driveway.

His mind clicked into gear. The shocked stupidity was gone. He was already running uphill. "I'm getting Geoffrey," he shouted over his shoulder, thinking that Chiffon drove, Chiffon would take one of the Aszlings' cars, and —

"I'll bring Egypt and Spice down here and tie them up to the front steps," said his sister. "There's enough pavement around they'll be fine there. Our grass is wet and we don't have propane, and we'll — "

"No, Danna! We've got to get out of the canyon. Chiffon will drive down and — "

His sister was a true Californian. "And forget it, Hall. We're staying with the house."

the Severyn house
4:05 P.M.

Beau remembered Elisabeth's Tarzan and Jane corner, where she tucked herself when Mom was being hardest on her. He ran down the driveway, following the paved switchbacks because he had to. The dusty gravelly canyon slopes were far too steep to climb, or even crawl.

"Elisabeth," he said rather than screamed, said in the voice of an adult who has had enough, who is going to turn you into the shape of a Lego block if you don't behave.

"I'm here," she said nervously, and he yanked her out of hiding with hands still so full of adrenaline it was like taking the door off its hinges again; he was afraid of his own hands and the roughness inside them.

"Ssshhhhhh, Beau." Elisabeth pointed toward the deer and the rabbit. They could have been garden sculptures, except that their flanks heaved for air. Nothing could have spooked Beau more than seeing wild animals too afraid of fire to be afraid of humans.

He couldn't wait for her to run; he picked her

up to carry her, which made Lizzie giggle in delight. She was rarely cuddled, and for her, this was a hug, not a rescue. She really was little, this eight-year-old. How could Mom possibly think of Elisabeth as chunky? He was aware of his sister's fragility and helplessness; she could have been the rabbit or the deer.

Beau ran up the hill. Fear of fire and lack of phone entered his legs and pumped them and he went up the hill as fast as he'd gone down, as if it were flat, as if his sister were weightless.

Beau set his sister down at the front door and they both giggled, as if he, too, were an eight-year-old girl. "Whew!"

"First, we've got to get sensible clothes on." Beau wore his favorite sneakers: plain high-top Converse, dark hunter green with white laces, except he hadn't laced them. He wore his favorite shorts, long and baggy as a gang member's trousers. A plain white T-shirt. Elisabeth had on white short shorts, a white tank top, and flimsy white sneakers. She was more bare than covered.

Beau had spent a good deal of his life caring for his skin: sunblock, lotion, oil, tanning to the special bronze so honored among men. He was proud of being physically impressive, had worked to get there, expected to work all his life to stay there. Beau was not willing to think of his skin charred.

"Put jeans on," he ordered, "and your heavy sneakers." Even as he said that he knew that they couldn't run up or down slickery hillsides in sneakers: they'd skid. They needed hobnailed boots. Beau did not happen to have a pair in his wardrobe. He thought briefly of his old baseball shoes, but he didn't know where they were, and they probably didn't fit anymore.

But they weren't going to run anywhere, anyway. Rescue trucks would be here momentarily, and meanwhile he and Lizzie just needed to keep wetting things down. If they did have to evacuate, they'd go by car, not on foot.

Grass Canyon Road
4:06 P.M.

The idea here was to drop a wet line.

Helicopters fitted with huge buckets made trips to the ocean, filling them with salt water. The buckets swung from chains like little kids in swings, way below the copters.

The sky was not a simple place to be right now, what with radio stations moving their helicopters in, and television stations getting their helicopters in, and the sheriff's department, and even some exceedingly wealthy and stupid homeowners renting helicopters to be flown in since the roads were blocked. Rising waves of heat could toss a plane around like a duckling in a hurricane. A crash landing into a firewall is not cool.

Tank engine crews and helicopters were after

the same thing: Wet it down, keep it back. But it was pointless here. If they kept at it, it was political: just to make the residents feel somebody was trying something. It wasn't going to make the fire feel anything.

This fire was above and beyond anything a mere drop of water could accomplish.

It was like a war, but not modern war. You couldn't chart the paths of a wildfire the way you could rockets. This was more like fighting Indians of old, never knowing from what thicket the arrows would fly.

Matt's goggles were too filthy to see out of, so he'd yanked them down half over his nose and mouth. He stood in a hazy fog of smoke. His partner was spraying mist to cool the air down around them, but it was just making a denser fog.

Uniforms were lime yellow, bandannas tied over mouths were triangles of red, gloves were white. Their helmets' lights were diamonds in a cave of smoke. The fire engines were parked face-outwards, so they could flee if it became necessary. Men wrestled with the dragon that was a water-filled hose, three of them fighting the strength of the water in order to use it on the strength of the fire.

This stretch of Grass featured glitzy residences amid wilderness as scrubby as backdrops for cowboy movies. Million-dollar houses lay below rough hills, dusty brown and full of tinder. Across the street, some moron homeowner actually thought he could drive eight cars out to safety. Listen, leave it this long, you weren't driving *one* car out.

His radio was full of half-decipherable reports coming from all over, ridden with static and interference. ". . . Pinch Canyon. It just blew."

My house! Matt clutched the little radio, as if the tighter he held it, the more he'd know.

He had grown up on Pinch Canyon.

He loved California: He loved the calendar year spiked not with holidays but with danger. He loved how southern California said to you — *I didn't ask you to come. I didn't promise safety.* How the land and climate fought back, waiting until you were relaxed and sure of yourself, then flinging in your face the proof that you were merely human.

In southern California, danger was what building was all about. Logical, rational people wouldn't dream of building in Pinch Canyon, which was a fire trap waiting for a hot, dry day and lots of wind and a vanity arsonist.

But, oh — the beauty! The harsh, demanding canyon walls, the azure blue sky, the distant slurred watercolory hills.

His parents' house, unlike every other in Pinch Canyon, was down in the bottom, among the oaks and ferns and vines. It was a house meant for pets and children: Matt and his sister and brother had had dogs and lambs and ponies and gerbils, endless supplies of cats, once a llama, and once a Vietnamese pig. His parents could hardly stand it on the weekends if everybody didn't have a friend sleep over, or two or three.

There were always relatives from out East, descending on the Marshes to enjoy Matt's sun and Matt's horses and Matt's canyon and Matt's beaches.

There was nobody home now during the day. Children and pets were long gone. But the watercolor his sister had done in first grade, the clay palm print Matt had done in kindergarten, these still held their places of honor and would be destroyed.

His parents would be okay, even if they lost everything. He supposed that memories would be okay, too: Nothing would damage the happy childhood he had had. But how he wanted the house and the oaks to survive!

Well, somebody else was fighting in Pinch. He was here. Matt swigged water from his belt canteen. The water was hot as coffee. His side pack held a silver blanket to be brought out if he faced death: He was to wrap himself in his own shroud. Then he'd just have to pray that man-made materials really did hold off fire and wouldn't instead just help cook him.

Some annoying girl without a brain kept wanting to talk with him. All he could say was, "Get out of here!" but she couldn't follow that instruction any better than anybody else.

A silver-and-red tanker plane spread fire retardant chemicals in front of the fire. On the ground, it was gaudy red, so firefighters could see where it had been dumped. "Of course, they can't spread it here," said June furiously, "because we have so many jerk homeowners who won't go, and they can't spray the stuff on people. If they'd just leave like they were told, we could save their houses!"

Did the blonde girl realize that "jerk" meant her? No, of course not, jerks were always other people. She smiled at him, as if they were on a date, or something.

"Morons," said June.

The girl kept smiling.

Los Angeles
4:07 P.M.

Courtney Azsling did not worry easily.

Fire? Earthquake? Thrown from a horse? Struck by a car? Felled by lightning? You could just as easily get hit by a falling asteroid or choke on a french fry. Stable, interesting people did not waste their time worrying.

Still, Courtney Aszling did wonder briefly if she should check to be sure that Elony and Chiffon had things under control. These fires seemed to be popping up everywhere, like revolutions in third world countries. But telephones were a problem. Elony hated the phone and let the answering machine take all calls, and Chiffon was usually with the baby, and didn't answer either.

Chiffon, she thought, shaking her head. Her parents probably meant to call her Siobhan and didn't know how to spell it, so the kid ended up named for a midwestern pie. Pitiful excuse for a name.

Courtney Aszling knew, because she was a judgmental woman, that Chiffon was also a pitiful excuse for a person, a truly lousy choice for your only child's caretaker, but it was hard to find full-time help that spoke English.

Before Drew and Courtney Aszling knew that being photogenic would be the only good thing about Geoffrey, they bought him a billion clothes. This was the best-dressed child in California, and that was something. But a year had gone by, and he'd outgrown his wardrobe twice, and now had only a fraction of the number of clothes. Who needed a wardrobe when nobody was going to take you anywhere?

This kid was sullen and unfriendly. He didn't say hi when his parents came in nor good-bye when they left. If Geoffrey didn't want to move, he didn't move. If he didn't want to eat, he didn't eat. If he didn't want to take riding lessons, he didn't get on the horse.

There was absolutely not one thing Geoffrey did unless he felt like it. Mostly, he felt like watching TV, wrapped in that repulsive purple velour, and sucking his thumb.

Courtney Aszling was so sorry she'd gotten sentimental about infants, swept up in this nonsense about biological clocks. She had a clock all right. Geoffrey was a little time bomb.

She thought gloomily of the next fifteen years. How early did boarding school start, anyway? In England, you could ship them off when they were six. Look at the little princes.

Now there was an idea. If it was right for the British royal family, it was surely right for her.

Courtney Aszling felt so cheerful about the boarding school possibility she forgot to check on anybody.

the Severyn house
4:08 P.M.

"Okay," said Beau, organizing himself. "Stay with me, Lizzie, or I'll get nervous. Now, we're going to use the swimming pool water to keep the house wet. This'll be a real adventure, Lizzie."

They crossed several rooms and emerged in the reflecting pool area, where green grass and tall cypress did not appear to have noticed a change in temperature.

"Beau, the deck is burning," said Elisabeth, pointing.

It was a tidy little burn. Beau focused the hose, dropped a steady stream of water on the knee-high flames, and it went out with a hiss of protest.

Elisabeth clapped. "Aw-right Beau! I get to do the next one."

The next one was a single splash of fire eating up the wood chips with which a flower garden was mulched. Beau was puzzled. "I thought those were soaking wet from the irrigation." He and Elisabeth got as close as they could and worked on the bonfire.

Beau thought he was facing the source of the fire. He did not stop to think how immense his house was, how it extended on several levels, blocking his view.

They whipped the bonfire and shook on it.

Elisabeth was thrilled to be partners with her big brother.

"I'm so thirsty," she said. "Firefighting is hot work. Let's get a Coke."

They turned, standing on a curve of the cement walk that wound among the cypresses, to find the house entirely enveloped in smoke.

the Luu Stable
4:08 P.M.

Last year after the mud slides, they couldn't even get to Pinch Canyon, because the Pacific Coast Highway was closed. Mud like hot brown lava had streamed across the road. What fascinated Danna was that it looked alive: It was no longer an inert object. It had plans — places to go, people to see, houses to destroy.

On the road into Pinch Canyon was a place so horribly eroded that Danna didn't like looking at it. It had been tortured, as if the hillside had once been alive, and the forces of mud and gravity and fire had ripped its living skin off, and left a scarred, dry, dead husk.

Somebody had sprayed it with grass seed, that queer greenish blue-gray color of the stickum that was supposed to keep the unsprouted seed from blowing off the dead hill. Danna didn't see how the poor little seeds were supposed to break through the crust and find good dirt for their roots. It seemed a lot to ask of one little teensy seed you could hardly even see in the palm of your hand.

Now she looked with approval at the reseeded areas on various parts of Pinch Canyon. They would be firebreaks, and at the pace at which firefighters were coming to rescue them, it looked as if Danna and Hall were going to need every firebreak they could get.

Where were the firefighters?

She could hear her father now, asking just what he was paying all these taxes for, anyway.

Oh, well, they'd be here any second. LA had fabulous fire departments, they were famous. Danna liked being from a place where everything was the best and everybody was famous.

She ran lightly up to the Luu stable. It was a cute little building, with curlicues carved on the eaves and doors. Egypt and Spice were in the paddock, circling and snorting and jigging anxiously. They wanted to get inside the stable, where they would feel familiar, and the fact that the stable was beginning to burn did not penetrate their little horse brains.

It did not occur to Danna to be afraid of Egypt or Spice.

She reached in the open stable door and grabbed the leads hanging there. It sure was a good thing she had gotten up here. The stable was going to bomb out the way that propane tank had, what with the hay and straw.

She spoke comfortingly to the horses and clipped the leads on their halters. They were not comforted.

I suppose, she thought resentfully, Hall will put up a fuss and we won't stay with the house. He'll make us go to the evacuation point. The local high school. How dumb. We won't have any fun that way.

She had not gone to public schools very long. Just first grade. Her room had had kids from Japan, Korea, Argentina, Armenia, Israel, Iraq, the Philippines, and, of course, immigrants from Oregon, Brooklyn, and Massachusetts. Of the twenty-nine children in her class, twelve didn't speak English at home. That was enough for her parents. Hall and Danna entered private school in only six weeks. Danna was always a little sorry. Even though she had great friends, loved her school, and was loyal to every decision her parents made, she wished she could have learned to talk to the kids from all those neat countries, and find out who was homesick and who was rich and who was smart and who was not.

In an instant, it became very clear who was smart and who was not.

The stable went with a blast of noise like the brass section of a symphony. Spice shuddered and plunged his head up and down, but Egypt, crazed with shock and fear, reared. His huge hoof, coming down, hit her in the shin, and she actually heard her bone snap.

"Oh, great work, Egypt."

She didn't fall only because she'd kept her grip on the leads, hanging onto them like trapeze ropes. She yanked the horses' heads down and for some reason this satisfied them so they calmed down a little, but she couldn't move. She couldn't put her weight on the broken leg. She couldn't mount either horse. She couldn't take a single step.

They stood there — horse, girl, and horse — while a hundred feet away, fire engulfed the stable, and turned the hay bales into ovens.

ARSON
WATCH

the Aszling house
4:08 P.M.

Geoffrey lay inside his blankie. He loved not being able to see anything. He loved the safe purple privacy. He loved his thumb and the hardness of the floor beneath him.

Only Elony was there, which was nice. She never tried to change him around. She'd fixed him a cup of milk with the little screw top, like a baby bottle but not really, so he could lie there and still drink. She lay on the floor with him and they were munching popcorn out of the same bowl.

His blankie was actually her velour, and his parents were always trying to make him give it back, but he knew Elony wouldn't make him. Elony understood that one possession could form the whole world. She never talked. She didn't try to assault him with her arms and hands and speech the way other people did.

Geoffrey wondered if Hall would come.

Geoffrey didn't care for speech. But Hall adored speech. If Geoffrey answered Hall just once, Hall laughed and clapped and did somersaults. Geoffrey wanted to somersault, and had

even thought about trying it, but mostly Geoffrey never tried anything.

Even Geoffrey, upon whom little had an im-
pact, sat up when Hall burst into the house
screaming. "Fire!" yelled Hall.

Geoffrey's velour fell down around his lap,
and he gathered it quickly. You never knew
when people would try to take something from
you.

"Come on!" screamed Hall. "Where's that
nursemaid? Where's Chiffon?"

Elony glared at him for being so loud and not
even knocking. "Chiffon take car. Errands," said
Elony.

"There's a fire," said Hall, grabbing at her.
"Come on."

Elony hated being plucked at, as if she were
frozen food. She didn't want to go with Hall. It
was bad enough she'd missed her bus. She didn't
want any other disruptions.

"Fine," said Hall. He grabbed Geoffrey, who
of course did not cooperate. The little boy rolled
over fast, cocooning himself into a fat purple
worm. When Hall struggled to lift Geoffrey, he
squirmed and made himself heavier. Geoffrey
remained mute, while Hall screamed and yelled.

To Elony, this frantic shoving was unpleasant.
She moved between the limp, silent purple child
and the hopping frenetic teenager.

"There's a fire!" shrieked Hall. "Don't you
understand?"

Elony shrugged.

Hall wanted to put a fist through her. What was with these people, shrugging when . . .

. . . when it dawned on him that the shrug didn't mean Elony was bored. It meant she didn't know the word *fire*.

Hall yanked open the heavy drapes and pointed.

The view should have been 3-D: closest, the baskets of pink and white fuschia edging the redwood deck; center, green oleanders growing below the deck; distant, Pinch Mountain silhouetted against a reliably blue sky.

Flowers, decks, and oleanders were the right colors in the right place. Pinch Mountain, however, was orange, and the spacious blue sky was black and white and seething all over with smoke.

"Fire," said Hall.

"Fire," repeated Elony. It was not a vocabulary word she was likely to forget.

Los Angeles
4:08 P.M.

Aden Severyn had not even waited for the valet to bring up his car. His heart pounded so hard he could barely think. Blood slammed around the corners of his body, screeching through his gut like bad brakes. His Mercedes, however, had excellent brakes. He left patches at every turn. If Beau did that, he'd take the kid's license away.

On the radio, the mayor said, "If you are a resident of Pinch Canyon, get out now. This is serious. Do not water your roof. Do not stop to find old photographs. Get. Out. Now."

Mr. Severyn could not believe what he was hearing. That fire was miles away! he thought. He was furious with the fire for moving so fast. Furious with fire departments for not preventing it better. Furious with himself for not listening to the news coverage — he whose world was news coverage — furious that nobody had told him about the shift in the wind.

He turned the radio volume way up. Sure enough, the mayor repeated himself. *This is serious. Do not water your roof. Do not stop to find old photographs. Get. Out. Now.*

I'm sure the sheriff's department already cleared Pinch Canyon. The kids're probably at some evacuation point already.

He grabbed his phone and called Beau. Nobody answered.

Was it ringing in a safely empty house? Or was it ringing amidst flames, his two children lying near it, suffocated by smoke?

He had a sudden whir of memory: an old black-and-white film playing without warning. How the year Elisabeth was two, he used to come home on time, running in the door, scooping her up in his arms, tipping her little body skyward and kissing her little nose as her tiny sneakers scraped the ceiling. He remembered her giggle of joy, her utter happiness that Daddy was home.

Aden Severyn made remarkable time for several miles by driving homicidally, cutting in and out with inches to spare.

Traffic slowed.

Traffic jams had never bothered this man. He was prepared. He had an excellent sound system. He had phone and fax. The soft vanilla leather and flawless, soundless air-conditioning were comforting, and when his foot was on the accelerator and his finger on the radio dial, the car was his kingdom.

He didn't even mind gridlock. He knew the city well, had his favorite local routes, and could bypass anything. Freeway blocked? So what? He knew five surface routes.

But today he knew nothing: not where the fire was, not where it had been, not where the roads were blocked. It was not acceptable to Aden Severyn to know nothing.

They were going thirty miles an hour, then twenty, then a crawl, and then nothing. Traffic closed, stitching the cars up like sutures on a wound. Mr. Severyn's car was not his best friend, but a monster, sealing him tightly inside with his favorite music.

Grass Canyon Road
4:09 P.M.

Chiffon loved the noise. It was like a great rock concert that had taken huge crews all night to set up. Fire kept hitting gas lines and propane tanks, and then tremendous explosions would send flame and shrapnel into the air.

The colors were stunning. Who could go back to a mere Fourth of July fireworks after a display like this? This was the kind of thing you wanted to see every year.

Chiffon was still provoked with the fireman who paid no attention to her, but he was still cute, so she was still working on him. "Get out of here!" the guy kept yelling, half at her and half at everybody else. He was cute when he was mad. "It's dangerous!"

Nobody even pretended to listen. They were mesmerized by the danger. It was impossible not to stare into the flames and the wreckage. The fire looked right back into Chiffon's eyes, willing her to stay. Chiffon was so hot she felt cooked. Poached. Done. Ready to serve. But she was in the center of the action now and would not consider backing off.

Fire reached the edge of the lawns.

The road would stop it. Asphalt would win.

Chiffon kind of admired the fire, over there on its side of the pavement. The fire acted like a tennis champ waiting for the first serve. On the far side of the road, the fire swayed and rocked, kept its ankles light and its legs limber.

At the exact moment it chose — with no regard for firefighters nor sightseers — it crossed the road. It ignored humans as the soles of shoes ignore ants. It left its droppings everywhere, like some huge hideous beast.

An ember the size of a doughnut fell into Chiffon's cupped fingers. She flung her hands up against her face, trying to protect herself, but had not yet dropped the ember, and she branded her own cheek. She screamed, and jerked back, but in the cacophony of the fire nobody heard the scream, and with the running and pivoting and wrestling everybody else was doing, nobody saw. The curtain of fire passed right over her, it felt as if it passed right through her, and yet she didn't burn, she was just knocked over, as if it had slugged her. What was the matter with the firefighters? They were supposed to keep the fire over there!

The fire, having crossed the road, progressed with an odd efficiency, skipping this house, grabbing that one, taking the top of one tree, leaving the next green and untouched. The burned side of the road was left black and twitching, like a corpse with a single living muscle left. Smoke rose to reveal houses that were already black skeletons, with a single garage, utterly untouched, its hanging baskets of ruby red geraniums still blooming in a friendly down-home way.

The firefighters regrouped, trying to cope with a new battleground.

"My face!" screamed Chiffon. She needed a doctor, an ambulance, immediate attention. "My face! I'm going to be an actress! I can't have scars on my face!"

Nobody listened.

She grabbed the cute fireman's arm, but instead of helping, he brushed her away like an insect and went on wrestling with a huge heavy hose.

She grabbed the arm of a woman leading dogs away from the conflagration and the woman snarled, just like her dogs.

People were so cruel. Chiffon couldn't believe it. There were ambulances someplace. She had to have one. She began running, trying to find an ambulance, she knew they were parked around here somewhere, but the smoke changed its mind and lowered itself back down, a thick stage curtain of smoke, and it was difficult to know where to run. She was no longer sure which way was out, and the faster she ran the deeper the smoke became, and the harder it was to breathe, and the more her burns hurt. She tripped hard over a curb, and fell into a little bonfire. Her bare kneecaps landed in charcoal briquettes, and she was seared, as if she were nothing but a steak on a grill. She managed to roll off, screaming, but nobody heard her, because the fire had gotten into somebody's gun cabinet, and hit the ammunition, and the neighborhood was literally being shelled, and everybody else was screaming too.

Grass Canyon Road
4:10 P.M.

Mr. Eight Cars had driven a romantic ancient battleship gray Rolls-Royce to the edge of his driveway. He couldn't get it out of the driveway because a firetruck blocked him. He was trying to get the firefighters' attention so they'd move their truck, but since the firefighters were using that truck to fight the fire on Mr. Eight Cars' own house, it seemed unlikely that they were going to drive off.

Mrs. Eight Cars had meanwhile packed a cute little teal blue pickup truck with stuff. Wrapped in towels or crammed in cardboard boxes, you couldn't tell what it was, but given the house it had come from, it had to be worth a lot. On top of it, she was throwing, loose, an enormous collection of photograph albums.

It was so hot, Swann felt like an ironing board, with somebody pressing her on the highest setting. The smoke was very annoying, the way it clouded up everything, so you could hardly see at all, or even breathe very well.

From the teal blue pickup, Mrs. Eight Cars

screamed at her husband, telling him to abandon the Rolls and its contents, to get in the truck with her, and they'd drive over the low brick walls and get out of here.

Hysterical people were such a kill. It seemed like the more money and possessions they had, the quicker they reached hysteria.

The contents of a Rolls-Royce, thought Swann, wondering what that might include.

Swann wondered for a moment if she and her parents ought to head back to the rental car. She had a funny uncomfortable feeling. What if fire trucks had blocked *their* car in? "Pop?" she said, but he'd already thought of it, and was backing their car closer to Eight Cars' to pick Swann up and get out of there.

The fire hopped the road.

"Hop" was perhaps not the word. Hop was a bunny word, a dance word.

This fire crossed the pavement as thick and rich as velvet drapery, embroidered in every flaming color. It was still burning even when there was nothing there but asphalt, which didn't burn. The fire maybe lay down on the road in order to cross it, Swann couldn't tell.

The piles and stacks of photograph albums that Mrs. Eight Cars had heaved into her pickup caught fire. Seconds later, she, her truck, and its gas tank were also on fire.

the Aszling house
4:10 P.M.

Elony soaked the purple blankie in water and wrapped Geoffrey in it. Geoffrey liked this: a bath without the tub. He was dripping and giggling. Even in this nightmare, Hall loved hearing Geoffrey giggle.

Hall held the wet kid in his wet blanket and he and Elony trotted down the twisted drive past the Luus' house. Danna would have the horses down at their house by now. Egypt and Spice couldn't have been half the trouble Elony and Geoffrey'd been.

There was so much noise. Windows breaking? Screams of glass? Tree trunks splitting? Bolts being yanked out of houses as burning decks fell a hundred feet down?

Worse than the noise by far was the heat. Hall doubted if the thermometers on his house even registered this high a temperature. They'd be dead if it got any hotter.

Halstead Press saw his own house start to burn. Fire on both sides of the driveway had eaten the burlap bags full of sand, leaving the sand in bag shape. Now it was joyfully consuming the trees that should not have been there because the Presses should have allowed nothing to grow so near the house.

Because of the air-conditioning, all windows were closed and the fire should have taken a while to establish itself. But no — Danna and

Hall had left the doors open. Packaged their house and handed it over.

He could not believe they had been so dumb! Who did they think Nature was? Some enfeebled old bag lady?

In only seconds, the preheated wood burst into flame.

The house was fully involved in barely a minute.

My home! he thought. Hall felt stabbed. The burning of his house smelled awful. He could taste poison gas. His contact lenses rasped cruelly on his corneas.

Danna was not there, so she'd given up her idea of saving the house, which was good, since there was no longer a house to save, and she and the horses must already be down in the road, waiting.

The box of kittens rocked back and forth as they struggled to free themselves. Hall motioned to Elony who grabbed it, and the handy six pack of Cokes on top. They rushed around the final hairpin turn. Below them, Pinch Canyon Road was empty. No Danna. No horses.

She wouldn't have ridden on ahead, would she? Danna, who wanted to stay with the house? She'd wait for Chiffon and the car and her own brother, wouldn't she? She couldn't know yet that there was no Chiffon and no car.

Elony said, "Geoffrey and I, we go."

"Wait," he said nervously. Smoke sat down over the shared hillside. Nothing was visible. It might have been an ocean of fog. "Danna!" he yelled, as if anybody could possibly hear anything in this din. "Danna, get down to the road! Hurry up!"

Elony wasted no more time. She set the kitten box down. She took Geoffrey, slinging the wet purple burden over her shoulder, ignoring any noises Geoffrey might be making. She set out for Pinch Canyon Road, or Grass Canyon Road, or the Pacific Coast Highway, or wherever she would have to go to get wherever she was going.

How solid her walk. As if she'd gone through fire in another life, and knew fire. Knew that if you just kept going, you would come out on the other side.

Hall ran back and forth, made stupid by the situation, not knowing whether to run after Elony or up to the Luus. Where was Danna? She should have left a note, or something.

He was swamped by panic.

This was how sons let their parents down; this was how sons did not end up doing great things.

Grass Canyon Road
4:11 P.M.

Swann and her parents did not even have to discuss it. They simply offloaded the contents of the Rolls into their rental car and drove away. In the chaos of the fire, the fire that weirdly spared this building or vehicle, and completely destroyed the one next to it, Swann's family was fine.

Mr. Eight Cars saw them.

He knew they were looters.

He knew he would recognize them again if they were caught.

He knew it didn't matter.

His wife, whom he had adored for forty-four years, was going to burn alive.

Grass Canyon Road
4:11 P.M.

Matt thought a Civil War battle, with cannon and muskets, must have sounded like this. He was deafened by horns and sirens, helicopter engines, house alarm systems going insane, and the fire itself, chewing, snapping, charring, breaking. Still, his ears registered a shriek of terror. Keeping the hose aimed at the roof, he turned only his head to see the source of the scream. Halfway through the turn, he saw the fire leap the road. Saw his own death.

The rest of the way through the turn he saw, swirling behind smoke, a white-haired woman in a blue truck enveloped in fire.

Matt pointed the nozzle toward the truck, trying at the same time to move toward her. He couldn't both handle the dragon of the hose and

walk forward. That was a three-man task. He
needed to signal his partners, but it turned out
not to be necessary.

The hydrants ran out of water.

the Severyn house
4:12 P.M.

Beau's thoughts were ripping out ahead of his
actions. I have to be sensible, he told himself, I
have to do the right thing.

He could think of nothing either sensible or
right.

He hung onto Elisabeth's hand so hard he was
afraid he would snap it off, and have only a hand,
and no Elisabeth.

It was such a nightmarish vision that he almost let go of her.

He tried to wet his lips, but his mouth was
too dry. They were on the cliff edge. From this
spot, they could not go around the house. Only
through.

Through fire!

"We have to go through the house, Lizzie,"
he said, picking her up.

"It's on fire!" she cried, fighting him, trying
to get back down and run. "We can't go in."

He tightened his arms on his sister to im-
prison her.

A window pane popped. The heat was too

much for the glass and it exploded, sending glass
splinters like shrapnel. Beau was stunned to see
cuts on his bare arms. They just appeared. He
saw nothing and felt nothing, but blood ran
heavily. "Are you okay, Lizzie?"

Her tears made wet spots on his chest. "Beau,
how are we getting out of here?"

He was so aware of her total dependence on
him; if he did not make it, she would not make
it. If he did not pull this off, she would not pull
this off.

His mind was loose. It felt like a pack of dangerous wild animals that had gotten away. It
wasn't doing anything civilized like thinking
things through and making plans, it was just
screaming *fire-fire-fire* and *get out — get out
get out.*

Bizarrely, his thoughts rushed to Michael, instead of fire or Lizzie or himself.

Stop this. Do something intelligent.

He could not tell if his mind or Michael's had
issued that instruction.

"It's only smoke, no fire yet," he said. "We
have to go that way. It's that or jump off the
cliff. Take a deep breath and don't breathe until
I tell you to." Pressing his sister to his chest, he
raced into the house.

No flames. At the ceiling, smoke floated like
fog.

Beau was a car person. He could not imagine
walking, jogging, running, or climbing except in
a fitness center. In the outdoors, the real world,

you drove. If they had a fire to escape, they also had a vehicle in which to do the escaping.

Either we make it by car, he thought, or we won't make it.

Not making it was not acceptable. He, Beau Severyn, was not going to burn to death. That was final.

Through the house he stumbled. It had never seemed so pointlessly large. Not breathing was a ridiculous order. Lungs didn't hold that much air. He made it to the kitchen just fine, though, and there among the white stretch of cabinets and counter, everything seemed completely ordinary. Everything except the ceiling, which was not flaming, but which was blackening, and curling up, and turning into charcoal as he stood beneath it.

No key hung on the hook at the back door, where they stuck tennis rackets, car keys, and messages. Feverishly he patted the counter. Magazines, mail, pocket calculator, pencils, videos, books.

No keys.

Vaguely, from safety lectures on television, he recalled that smoke was more dangerous than flame. He had to get Elisabeth where she'd be breathing good air.

"We'll jump the car going downhill," he said briefly, and shoved Elisabeth ahead of him into the garage. He flung her into the passenger seat and reached over her to the remote control clipped to the visor.

The remote didn't work.

The automatic doors did not move up.

Beau couldn't believe it.

The doors didn't open.

If he had a car key, he'd just back the Suburban right through the doors, but he had to get the vehicle on a slope in order to jump it, had to get it rolling, couldn't do that in the garage.

Elisabeth was like a stick figure on the big front seat. She was looking at him with huge terrified eyes, waiting for him to save her, expecting him to save her.

He had to find those car keys. Praying that he had another few minutes to play with, Beau fumbled for the knob of the connecting door between the garage and kitchen. He had forgotten to adjust the lock.

They were locked out.

Sealed in the garage.

NO
OUTLET

Grass Canyon Road
4:12 P.M

Matt was horrified.

One moment he had water, the next moment he didn't.

One moment the hose was a living, bucking animal of tremendous strength, and the next moment it was just limp canvas.

He shook it, as if that last drop of water were the one that would put the fire out.

The little truck was still on fire.

The husband, forgetting his cars, figuring the truth out at last (possessions don't matter a lot if your life is over) was unable to reach his wife. The fire was far, far too hot to thrust his bare arm through the flames to grab a handle, which was actually changing color as it heated.

Dropping the worthless hose, Matt Marsh moved forward into the searing oven of the fire to grab the handle of the teal blue truck.

His huge thick gloves were protection, but not as much as he expected them to be. He felt the heat enough to want to scream and let go, but he didn't. My fingers are burned, he thought. Please, God, don't let me lose my fingers. He yanked the door open and reached in for the woman. She was ready and climbed on him like a monkey to a tree. Staggering back, grateful that she was light and slender, Matt looked through filthy goggles to see where to go.

The fire was roaring on all sides, eating everything except what it melted. The tires on the pickup were melting.

Nice, thought Matt Marsh.

The fire had circled them. In the great wrestling bout, it was going for the final round. They were going to roast like meat.

Desperately distributing themselves among trucks, while houses on each side burst into flames of inky black and evil orange, June and his partners had made it into the cabs, hoping to wall the fire off at least a little bit. Everybody knew stories of firefighters who had been burned right through the metal doors.

Matt could not get there.

He had to use the house itself for safety.

Houses usually burn slower than brush or trees. If they could make it inside, maybe they could flatten to the floor, find a little oxygen, and maybe the fireball would burn on by. Then they'd try to get out of the house and make a run to where the fire was finished, before the house did burn down around them.

Of course, that game plan didn't always work. This fire was so hot that houses were almost combusting spontaneously. If that happened now, Matt would learn what it is to burn alive.

He gambled on the house because there wasn't another gamble around. He bent, shoved up, and slung the woman onto his shoulder. The husband stuck close without needing to be told and they ran inside the burning building.

Pacific Coast Highway
4:13 P.M.

Mr. Severyn was as mired in traffic as if there had been a mud slide after all. A line of bright yellow bulldozers was being pulled up the Pacific Coast Highway on flatbed trailers. They would unload to carve up the earth, turn dirt on top of anything flammable, and build instant firebreaks. Nobody was going to go anywhere until that line of trailers got through. And all that time, his children would be alone and in danger.

I don't know any of my neighbors, he thought, and they don't know me. I never wanted to. I don't care about a neighborhood, I care only about my own family, my own house, and my own land.

Who will know that my children are alone? Who will know that somebody has to look out for them? Who will think to go up that drive and be sure that Beau and Elisabeth are out?

He remembered the ugly town of his childhood. How gladly he'd left the empty steel mills and the damp icy climate. But he had left behind the only true neighbors he'd ever had: On that street, somebody would have thought to check on the elderly and remember the young.

He remembered the son for whom he had not been a father or a neighbor. Was this payback? Was this destiny — his loved children in trouble because he had not bothered to love the first one?

Oh, Michael, he thought. Then he jumped out of the car and jogged alongside a trailer, asking the driver where they were headed.

"Command Post on Grass Canyon."

"Can you give me a ride?"

"No, sir. Sorry. Against the rules."

The Severyn family had an unusual habit of using cash instead of credit. Mr. Severyn thought this might be a useful time to mention this habit, or at least open his wallet and display it.

The flatbed driver agreed that Mr. Severyn could ride with him after all.

Grass Canyon Road
4:14 P.M.

Matt was right. The exterior of the house was on fire, but the interior was just smoky. Of course, smoke equaled poison and death, but if they lay low there might be enough oxygen. He and the two old people flattened beneath the silver protective blanket.

He kept in communication with June by radio, which was weird. He was going to be able to keep up a running dialogue of his death, unless of course he suffocated as he talked.

"We're calling in paramedics," said June. "Hang in there, Matt, you did the right thing."

Fire was up in the ceiling. The room began raining fire.

"We're kind of in trouble here," said Matt.

This was an understatement, and it made the elderly man laugh. Matt liked the laugh; it was a survivor sound, a good sound.

"I think you're going to be able to leave pretty quick," said June, which was fine for her to say; it wasn't raining fire on her back. "This fire is moving at an incredible rate. I've never seen anything like this. The wind is taking the whole fire with it. Keep low, keep calm, you can walk out in a few minutes."

Calm sort of isn't in the picture if your skin is burning. It was not a three-person blanket.

Behind them, the draperies caught fire. Yellow heat flashed around the room and then, surprisingly, died.

He wondered how quick death was, and if he would know about it, or if it would just flash through him like that, and he would no longer be there — only the charred flesh that had once been Matt Marsh.

"Let's run to the garage," said the old man. "It can't burn, all it can do is get hot enough to melt us."

"Hey, I'd rather melt any day," said Matt, and he swung the woman up again and they ran, crouched and terrified, through blistering smoke, and Matt, at least, knew that to breathe this nonair was to die.

the Severyn house
4:14 P.M.

It was sobering to see how easily panic had taken over. A matter of seconds, and Beau's thinking had deserted him. He was more shocked to learn that he, Beau Severyn, could panic than he was shocked at the fire.

All he had to do to open the garage door by hand was raise the overhead arm from its connection, and lift upward. Sure enough, the garage door proved rather light and slid easily into its storage slot on the ceiling.

Because of the large, paved, turnaround for the cars, there was no fire in front of him.

"There's a spare car key in a little metal box under the driver's seat, Beau," said Lizzie.

He knew that. He had put it there. "Thanks, Lizzie." He was very glad she hadn't seen him lose every molecule of common sense.

He slid behind the wheel, as relaxed and leisurely as if they were headed for school, and she fished out the little box and handed him the key, and he said Do you have your seatbelt on? and she said Yes she did, and he drove out of the garage.

Beau gave his beloved house a last look. It seemed okay except for the places where it was burning. Minor places, places you could get with a hose, and things you could . . .

. . . *things you could save.*

His hands continued to steer.

His feet braked, his eyes focused, and his concentration didn't give way.

But his heart gave way. The terrible loneliness that assailed him whenever he thought of Michael came again. Dying without your father's love was worse than dying of smoke.

Oh, Michael! he thought. I can't leave you there, as if you don't matter.

He tried to talk to the brother he had never known, arguing, as if there had ever been talk, let alone arguments; or maybe he was arguing with Dad. Or with disease. Or with death.

Elisabeth, he said to himself, Lizzie is first, she can't die either. I have to save my sister and then I can go back for my brother.

Go back for my brother.

This seemed brilliant to Beau, a good solid knight-in-shining-armor thought.

He maneuvered down the tight switchbacks. The fire was haphazard, strewn like confetti after a wedding. He had to drive over some fire.

It definitely gave him pause. What if fire somehow got into the gas tank?

Don't be ridiculous, he said to himself, the underside of the Suburban is not cardboard.

The driveway was very narrow, some space taken up by rows of sandbags, because everybody on Pinch Canyon had thought that mud slides were going to be the problem this year, and he had little room in which to maneuver. Twice he had to drive the very tires through flame — burning treetops thrown into the drive by the wind. What if the tires melted, or the sharp, splintered branches gave him a flat? The idea of changing a tire in the middle of Pinch Canyon right now actually made him laugh.

Around the next switchback, an unidentifiable burning object filled half the driveway. Its flames were higher than the Suburban, so brilliant he had to squint, and he had no idea what it was that was actually burning. In any event, he didn't want to drive into it.

They had the windows down and he pushed the button that raised them. He felt oddly less safe with the windows closed, as if he had constructed a coffin instead of an escape route.

Time to test the Suburban.

He drove half onto the high, cut-in-the-hill side of the driveway, his right wheels tilted up the wall instead of flat on the road, and then he accelerated, rocketing past the danger at such an angle they might just tip over and land in the very fire he wanted to avoid, but they didn't, and he hit the next switchback far too fast. They missed going over the edge by very little, instead knocking a whole row of sandbags down into the canyon below.

His little sister clapped. "Oooh, Beau, you're such a good driver! This is such fun."

And it was.

Beau had never had so much fun. Not scuba diving off Australia, not backpacking in the Rockies, not exploring volcano rims in Hawaii.

This was pretty neat. Of course, they were going to lose the house. But as his dad and every neighbor always said, these are the risks you take to live in paradise.

Beau and Elisabeth began laughing with a sort of weird delight. They were having a real adventure. Not a fake, travel-agency type adventure, not a pay-lots-of-money-and-get-a-little-nervous-while-your-guides-protect-you type adventure. The real thing.

Pinch Canyon
4:14 P.M.

Elony desperately wanted another cigarette. How funny, when she was going to die from smoke, that she still ached to fill her lungs with it on purpose.

Fires hitting the wiring of the houses on Pinch Canyon touched off alarm systems. The screeching of burglar alarms echoed and reechoed through the canyon.

Elony assumed that this ugly racket would bring rescuers rushing into Pinch Canyon.

Pinch Canyon people were rich. They would have left nothing to chance. Although everything had gone wrong up there on the hillside, down here on the road, everything would be right.

So even though she was terrified, walking toward Grass Canyon with a dripping purple burden on her shoulder and fire on both sides, she was not actually worried.

the health club
4:14 P.M.

Wendy finished blow-drying her hair and paid careful attention to her makeup. In order to stay young and lithe and perfect, she worked her muscles hard. After exercise, however, it was key to look as if she never dreamed of exercise, as if this beautiful body was a gift.

"Mrs. Severyn? Mr. Severyn is on the phone for you," said one of the attendants, smiling, and handing her a portable phone.

"Hello, darling," said Wendy Severyn, fastening an earring.

"Wendy, they evacuated Pinch Canyon. I don't know if the children are all right."

The bottom fell out of everything. She felt as if she had lost her heart and lungs and the soles of her feet, as if even her brains were sliding down into the vortex. "They didn't answer the beeper?" she said. They always answered the beeper; that was the point; that was why you had beepers.

"Wendy, try to get through from your direction. I've hitched a ride from the south, but you're north of them, maybe the roads aren't as jammed up there. Get in the car. Now."

"But where shall I go?" she cried. "If they've evacuated Pinch — "

"I think the high school is the evacuation point. I'll head for Pinch, you head for the high school. We'll keep calling each other and one of us will find the children."

He disconnected. Just like that, with no details, no comfort, no nothing, Aden was gone. She handed the phone back to the attendant without seeing her.

Beau, she thought. *Oh, Beau!*

Wendy Severyn had no use for guilt. Guilt and worry were bad for your complexion, your sleep, and your peace of mind.

So she told herself it was not guilt she was feeling, this sick mud slide of emotion at the bottom of her soul.

She did not want their beautiful wonderful house burned. She did not want one molecule of her life changed, except maybe for Elisabeth to be more acceptable. She resented the fire for touching *her* part of the world; and when she walked outdoors and saw the evil black sky, and

the orange sunset where the sun was not setting,
and choked in the particle-laden air, and had to
use the windshield wipers to remove ash before
she could drive — well, really!

She drove fast, lips in a pout.

I know they're all right. They have to be all
right. If they're not all right, it won't be my fault.
Nobody can blame me, nobody can say I didn't
do my best.

But nobody had said.

The only person saying that was Wendy herself.

The windshield wipers of her mind cleared her
thinking painfully and hideously.

I didn't do my best, she thought.

the Luu house
4:14 P.M.

Danna had plenty of time to study the fire.

The fire seemed to study her right back, like
a thief planning how to break in and what to
take.

Spice had jerked back and this time Danna
had let go of the lead, afraid of where Spice
would land. The horse moved sideways, jittering
around, and then he bolted. There was not one
thing Danna could do except hope that Spice
went away from the fire and not toward it.

Should she let go of Egypt, too, and let him run? She felt better hanging onto him; he was company. She could not bear to die alone.

It was strange to be fourteen and know you were going to die. Like Joan of Arc, you were going to be burned at the stake. There was no stake here, though. No ropes tying her up. Not even a pile of sticks around her feet to which her enemies were setting fire.

Danna had been her own enemy.

She was so afraid that fear gave up and melted and she was not afraid. She was simply waiting.

She tried to move the broken leg, but it didn't obey her.

She tried to fall over and start crawling, but the pain when she changed position was so great she couldn't make herself do it. This isn't logical, she said to herself. Any pain is better than death by burning. Think how painful that will be!

Let go of Egypt, she ordered herself. He's doomed, standing with me. He'll run. He's huge. Fast. He can run over fire or through it.

She forced herself to unwrap her clenched fingers from the leather rope. Egypt did not appear to notice this and stayed right where he was. I could give him a good whack, make him run, she thought. But her body didn't do it. The arm she needed to extend wouldn't allow her to lose her balance like that.

She thought she saw Hall coming. In the swirl-

ing smoke, like a curtain with holes in it — *now
you see me, now you don't*, it snickered — he
seemed to take a long time. Or else, more likely,
he was a mirage of pointless hope.

"Where," said Danna Press out loud, "is an
ARMED RESPONSE when you really need one?"

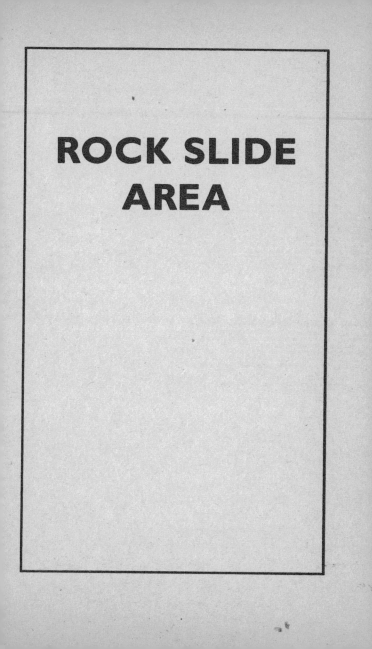

ROCK SLIDE AREA

the Luu house
4:15 P.M.

Hall heard her through the smoke. "Yo!" he shouted. "Armed Response! Where are you?"

"Right here!" his sister shrieked.

She was, too, right there. The smoke was so thick he had not been able to see her only a few yards away. What happened to the paddock fence? he thought, confused because he had expected to find it as a landmark. Then realized the fire had already eaten it. His feet weren't burning off because the constant use of the paddock by Egypt and Spice had killed any grass, so it was bare ground, and had offered no fuel. Fire was all around them, but only knee-high, and not actually on top of them, and the driveway, at this moment, still offered a path.

Not a safe path, but a path.

He waved his arms windmill fashion, as if he thought he could sweep the smoke away from them, and it was a major error, because Egypt, already terrified, went berserk at the churning arms suddenly appearing in his face. The horse reared, not whinnying so much as screaming, high and long like an engine whistle, not a horse, and then he ran. His sweaty filthy flank brushed hard against Hall, but Hall was more shocked by how hot the horse's hide was than how close he'd come to getting run over by the neighbor's horse.

His sister was just standing there, as if the fire had turned her to stone. That terrified him more than the fire or the bolting horse, and that was saying something.

"I broke my leg," said Danna conversationally. She was hoarse from smoke, as if she'd been screaming for hours. "Egypt kicked it."

He couldn't worry about Egypt and Spice now. "Which leg?"

She pointed.

Hall was nine inches taller than Danna but he was still adolescent thin. He hoped, prayed, that he was adult male strong. Adrenaline turned out to be pretty neat. He squatted slightly, his back to Danna, grabbed her thighs and lifted. Then he adjusted his hips until she was sitting okay on his butt. When she stopped screaming, he started walking. The damaged leg didn't look that bad, sort of like two knees on the same leg, but no bleeding. It was the scream that was awful, torn out of Danna's lungs and lasting until he thought he would throw up.

When the screams ended, she leaned on top of him, hunched and panting. More animal than person: heaving lungs and hanging tongue. She was hideously heavy. He could not believe a small person could be so heavy. He thought of the distance down the driveways, and the fire closing in, and the lack of cars.

He resolved to think of nothing but lifting his feet. He would not pay attention to the weight on his back, any more than the horses would have paid attention to it. Lifting feet was the thing, putting them ahead of each other, as far ahead as his knees would allow.

Somehow they passed the carcass of his own house, without Hall's back or mind breaking. Somehow they turned the final switchback and somehow he knew he would make it to the canyon bottom. Don't think about what's down there, he said to himself. Don't think. Thinking's bad. Feet. Lift feet.

"The kittens," gasped his sister. "Hall, get the kittens."

Like he could almost bend over and pick up a carton of kittens.

He tried to tell her that was ridiculous, he hardly had enough oxygen to manage his feet with, these things happened, and there you were, but he found he could not carry his feet past the kittens either. Somehow he curled even tighter in the spine and somehow found the strength to close his fingertips on the box and tuck it against his stomach. Danna's hands roped his throat, her one knee bit into his side, her broken leg hung stupidly, and the kittens found the oxygen Hall wanted for himself, and screamed huge kitten screams for freedom.

His feet had memorized their pattern and his mind returned to thinking and suddenly, he could not believe how much there was to think about. Elony and Geoffrey — were they making it to Pinch Canyon Road okay? What other families were home? Who had a car? Who would pick them up? Where were the rescue vehicles? Could a helicopter land in this? How bad was it at the mouth of Pinch? If they got out on Grass, would they be okay? How long would his back stand this? If his back gave in, what would he do? Drag his sister? Could they do a three-legged march?

Pinch Canyon
4:16 P.M.

At the bottom of the driveway, Beau paused like a normal driver in a normal situation and looked left and right.

To the left was a scurrying little Hispanic woman carrying a purple rug.

To the right —

There are other people here! thought Beau, sick that he had forgotten — *completely* forgotten — that his was not the only family on Pinch Canyon Road. Some housemaid was trying to outrun the fire.

He turned right, *away* from the woman.

Elisabeth screamed, "Beau! You monster! We have to get her!"

"We are getting her! Calm down. I'm going to

back up. I don't want to be facing the fire. I want to be facing the exit. I'm just being sensible." A purple rug, thought Beau. Now I ask you. With all the things you could save . . .

He accelerated very quickly, far faster than he had ever backed a car or even seen a car backed, and the woman moved into the half-burning scrub at the edge of the road to wait for him.

Elisabeth slid over the back of the seat and opened the door for the woman.

The purple rug was sopping wet.

When the maid unrolled it, it contained a beautiful little boy.

It was that creepy little Aszling kid. The adoption that failed.

And I thought she was saving a piece of carpet, thought Beau, ashamed. I couldn't even find car keys, and she's out there saving a life.

The woman was too tired to lift the little boy, so Beau put the car in Park and raced around the vehicle to help them both in.

"We wait," said the woman.

Words throbbed in his skull like stunted basketball cheers. *Drive-drive-drive! Go-go-go! Fire-fire-fire! Run-run-run!*

She was just a girl, his own age. Extremely pretty. Thick straight black hair half up in some sort of knot and the rest like a ribbon down her back. Enormous eyes, like a painting on velvet of a waif by the side of a road.

"We're not waiting," said Beau. He put the

Aszling kid in the center seat and strapped his seat belt on. The fire was not so scary when you were actually driving and it felt as if you were escaping. But fumbling with seat belts and wasting valuable oxygen on pointless discussions, it felt as if the fire were a murderer with a submachine gun already aimed.

"Wait for Hall and Danna," explained Geoffrey.

"Why, Geoffrey, I never heard you talk before," said Elisabeth, delighted.

Beau was sick with urgency. Gale force winds were filling the canyon now. The fire's heat was lifting sleeves and hair as if there were going to be a hurricane. *"Hall and Danna Press are still in their house!"*

Geoffrey nodded. "Horses."

"Whose horses?" screamed Beau. He could not lower his voice. He knew that panic was going to come inside him through the door of his shrieking.

"Egypt and Spice," said Geoffrey.

Beau all but threw the Hispanic girl into the car, too, and then he raced around the Suburban once more, got in the driver's seat, and still in reverse, aimed for the Press-Luu-Aszling driveway.

Well, Hall and Danna might have gone to get Egypt and Spice, but the horses had made their own choice. They came galloping out of the smoke, one after the other, passing so close to the Suburban that Beau couldn't even be sure the horses had seen the vehicle.

Blind with fear, thought Beau, trying to fend off the same feeling.

The uninhabited side of Pinch Canyon was not so bad. A few trees that clung to the rock-faces and some scrub a foot or two high were burning away, but not killer burning, just burning burning. But on the inhabited side, the fire was moving so fast! It was taking great, bus-long strides, and here he was, with sister, toddler, and maid, going back into it.

Good practice, he reminded himself.

Elisabeth was chatting away. "What's your name?" she said cheerily. How partylike, how hostessy, she sounded: just the way Mom was always coaching her to address guests.

"Elony."

"Oh, that's pretty," said Elisabeth.

We're going to get killed here, thought Beau, and she's deciding if names measure up to her standard.

The Luu house — and presumably Danna and Hall — was in the middle of a very steep drive-way. Beau wasn't sufficiently skilled to back up those tight curves, but neither did he dare go frontward. If the fire trapped them, he could never turn around.

He'd have to park down here and wait for them. Wait when fire was flashing like lightning only a football field away?

His thoughts were getting out of control again, racing off little side avenues, now when he needed every thought focused.

Panic, said Beau sternly, as if Panic were a gang member and he was going to talk Panic out of attacking him. Panic, beat it.

Pinch Canyon Road
4:17 P.M.

Transportation!

Hall recognized the Severyns' Suburban. Elony was waving from the window. Hall did not have enough oxygen to shout, but he didn't need to. Beau backed the Suburban right up to him, leaped out of the driver's seat, and took the box first.

"Kittens," said Hall. "Give 'em to Elisabeth."

Beau obeyed, and Elisabeth was delighted, crooning to the kittens through the frayed and stretched cardboard holes.

Danna sagged on Hall's back. Her complexion was a sort of olive white, a color from the vomit end of the spectrum. He eased Danna off Hall, and Hall remained bent, unable to fix his spine, while Danna moaned horribly. From inside the car, Elony grabbed Danna's shoulders, turned her, and sat her on the floor of the car. Beau lifted her legs, trying to distribute her pain carefully, and together, he and Elony slid Danna backward into the vehicle. The Suburban was, after all, as long as an ambulance.

It seemed to Hall that they spent hours doing this, precious precious time, while the fire advanced.

"What happened?" cried Elisabeth.

"She broke her leg," said Hall. He had managed to straighten. Beau ripped open the front passenger door and bundled Hall in. Hall began doing back calisthenics to ease the muscles.

The fire was bounding forward, skipping houses, as if it saw tastier morsels. How does it skip? thought Beau. It isn't playing fair.

Elony splinted the broken leg with the sopping wet velour. Danna was not crying. Maybe it was so hot that her tears had dried up; she was dry-crying. Elony popped open one of the Cokes and dribbled soda into Danna's eager mouth.

Beau slammed the gas pedal to the floor and the heavy Suburban with its tremendous engine roared down Pinch. Then immediately Beau backed off and drove slowly. "Hall, can you drive?" he said.

"I don't have a license."

"Who cares about a license? Can you drive?"

"Yes."

They had reached the Severyn driveway. A little distance, not much, was between them and the major fire. Way up its scenic driveway, the Severyn house was smoking. Low easygoing flames were consuming its decks. The fire status of the house had not changed. He could still get

in. "Good. You drive. I have to get something."
Beau put the car in Park and vaulted out.

Hall stared at Beau. "What are you doing?"
Hall felt entirely blank, the way you felt when
the VCR failed and instead of being inside the
movie, you were suddenly inside some TV chan-
nel; all new characters in all new dialogue starting up without a split second's notice.

"Go on without me," said Beau. "I have to get
something."

Go on without him?

Far ahead of them, going around the final
curve of Pinch Canyon, one of the two horses
was momentarily visible, dark and beautiful like
a statue seen through the fog. The horses were
the only sensible ones around: They knew
enough to leave.

"What are you talking about, Beau? Get back
here!" Hall screamed at Beau, unable to believe
his ears. Beau was going back into the burning
house?

"Drive on!" yelled Beau over his shoulder. He
was actually running uphill with a sort of ea-
gerness on his face, as if he had a mission. "I'll
be okay."

How could he be *okay?* There was nothing
okay about what he was doing. Where did this
word *okay* come from?

Swear words poured out of Hall: He was like
a dictionary of obscenities. "Beau! Get back
here! You'll get killed! Your house is on fire!
Stop!"

But Beau disappeared, taking the switchback, the thickets of undergrowth that sheltered deer and rabbits hiding him from sight.

The gas line that fed the houses on Pinch was barely beneath the dirt, and back at the Press-Luu-Aszling driveway it was not beneath the dirt at all, but just lying there, between the roots of trees and weeds. The fire was so hot it melted a weld and the pipe exploded. A long, steady stream of gas burned blue and white.

Hall assumed that the fire would work its way down the pipe, or that the heat would explode the entire length of the pipe, or that the pipe would continue to supply gas to the fire, which would fill the entire canyon. Either way, they were going to burn.

"Beau!" he bellowed, one more time. "Stop! Get back here!"

Pinch Canyon
4:18 P.M.

Hall found himself behind the wheel with no memory of having shifted from the passenger side.

How could Beau do this to me? How could he put me in the position of abandoning him? Because that's what I have to do. I have to drive away.

Hall hated Beau right then, hated him with

passion he had not experienced in all his fifteen years.

Hall put the car in Drive.

"No!" screamed Elisabeth. "Wait for my brother!"

"Hall, there has to be some way we can wait for him!" shrieked Danna.

"How can we wait?" shouted Hall. "The fire isn't waiting! The fire didn't say, 'Oh, okay, I get it, you need a twenty-minute intermission, hey, sure.'"

They were all screaming, the Suburban was practically rocking from the volume of their screaming, and the fire screamed, too. The wind increased and through the open window it lifted Hall's hair in a gust that roasted his skin.

"No, no, no, no, no!" cried Elisabeth.

With all the racket around them, he could still separate out her lungs, heaving like a scared animal's, like the flanks of the deer coursing out of the hills.

"You can't drive away and leave him here!" yelled Danna from the floor. "There isn't any way for him to get out but us."

Beau Severyn had selfishly, for utterly unfathomable reasons, forced Hall into a hideous corner. Could Hall really and truly put his foot down on the accelerator and drive away, and leave Beau to certain death? He had stopped for kittens. Could he refuse to stop for Beau? But the flames — the gas line — the heat of just the wind, never mind the fire itself — everything was gaining on them, at a horrific pace.

Hall had just become the oldest. The driver. The one in charge. He had more lives to think about than just Beau's. If he had to sacrifice the stupid one in order to save the group, then he had to.

In that moment, Halstead Press knew that he had grown up, and that Beau had not, and that being the grown-up was not cool.

It was a terrible burden.

Pinch Canyon
4:18 P.M.

The pain was unbelievable. Danna honestly could not believe that anything could hurt so much. She could not believe that she, Danna Press, *she* was a burden. She was the kind of person who did everything, and did it well, and did it right the first time. Now she was nothing but a nuisance, a jerk who had to be carried?

And Beau — what was he doing? She couldn't see from here. She screamed, "What is he doing, Hall? Don't let him, Hall! Make him come with us."

It was hard to think through the pain.

But she would rather have pain than be held responsible for Beau dying. How could Beau be so selfish, so crazy? How dare he put them in this position?

Running back into the fire?

A wash of horror came over Danna. Ice, when she was dying of heat exhaustion. It was nauseating, to freeze when she was baking. I am of no use, she thought. And Beau — he's worse.

Her brother drove on. How horrible to be flat on the car floor, unable to see, unable to imagine what Beau could be doing, or heading into, or why. And the horses. Danna would just have to trust them to the kindness of strangers.

Elisabeth was shrieking incoherently, trying to battle her way out of the Suburban. There was a little latching sound, as Hall hit the mechanism to lock all doors.

Beau will die, thought Danna. We're abandoning him.

But not really.

He abandoned *escape.* He chose this. It's his own stupid fault.

Oh, Beau, Beau! How could you be so dumb?

Pinch Canyon
4:18 P.M.

Elisabeth stopped screaming because everybody screamed right back at her for screaming.

Her very own adored brother would be a fire ghost. Another mysterious death, for reasons nobody would ever know. Beau, like the ghost of the stables, was willingly walking into fire.

Beau! she thought, drawing the syllable out in a desperate loss and fear. *Beauuuuuuuuuu.*

In her terror, Elisabeth cuddled Geoffrey. They were actually not so far apart: ages four and eight. She was closer in age to Geoffrey than to Danna, who was fourteen. And Danna right now was closer to pain than anything else.

Elisabeth was only eight, but eight is pretty old. Old enough to know that if her parents had to lose one of their two children, they would not want it to be Beau.

She wanted Beau to live because she loved her brother.

But she wanted Beau to live because otherwise her parents would wish that she had been the one to die.

It was too big and ugly a thought for anybody, least of all anybody eight years old.

There was plenty of purple velour to go around even after it was splinted on Danna's leg, and since Elisabeth had to have a hiding place for her tears, she wept inside the soft, hot, soaking wet fluff of the blankie.

It seemed to Elisabeth that Geoffrey cuddled back. Maybe she was pretending, because she was so desperate, but she felt that somehow he knew Elisabeth was worse off than he was. They clutched each other, while the Suburban lurched because Hall, who *could* drive, but certainly *hadn't,* found out that the accelerator was very responsive.

"It's okay," said Elony to Elisabeth, because Americans liked this phrase, whether or not it proved to be the case.

Why, Elisabeth needed to know, why had Beau gone back?

Her brother had many possessions, and few mattered to him. He was not in love with his things. There was no baseball card collection, no favorite trophy, no beloved anything Beau wouldn't just shrug about and buy another.

He'll die, thought Elisabeth, and become nothing, but always there, like the stable ghost. Fingers stretching out and never finding. He'll live in the ashes of our house, and —

And she knew what he had gone back for.

For something that was nothing, and was everything.

Grass Canyon fire
4:18 P.M.

"You have to help me!" shrieked Chiffon.

"Listen, lady," said the EMT, "we got people that are burned. We don't have time for you."

"Look at me!" screamed Chiffon.

"You fell down!" shouted the EMT. "Stop bothering us. We got people that are *really* hurt."

"I'll sue you!" she sobbed.

"Fine. Feel free. Just get out of the way."

Chiffon could not believe it. They were not going to treat her? This was America! How dare they tell her to beat it! What did they think their job was?

She sobbed and patted her burned hands and cheeks, felt the scorched edges of her hair and stared at the charred clothing that had protected the skin beneath it.

Nobody paid the slightest attention to her. The fire passed on.

The filth of disaster covered Grass Canyon Road.

Some houses were untouched: lawns still emerald green, tennis racket still balanced by the door.

Next door would be a black hole, smoke hanging waist-high above what had once been a house. A piece of sofa, a shoe, a briefcase: These sat in the ashes as if somebody had added them after the fire.

The ambulances treated some fireman for smoke inhalation, which really annoyed Chiffon. Weren't burns that were going to scar a beautiful girl's entire future more important than some fireman's lungs, for heaven's sake? They treated some old couple whose clothes and hair had burned off. Chiffon didn't like having to look at this; it was indecent. They should do it inside the ambulance where you didn't have to see. But everybody insisted the inside of the ambulance was full.

I bet, thought Chiffon, resentfully. Now she recognized the fireman on the stretcher. The really cute one who had brushed her off like a bug. Well, he wasn't really cute now.

The fireman coughed and whispered, "Is it true that Pinch Canyon is completely gone?"

"We don't have full information on that yet," said somebody to the fireman.

It was the kind of answer for when you don't want to upset somebody with the truth. Pinch Canyon — gone?

Gone?

But Geoffrey . . .

Chiffon was suddenly very glad she had lied about her name and age when she got the job on Pinch Canyon. Very glad neither Mr. nor Mrs. Aszling had ever asked for a social security number, since they didn't want to pay their share, because she would be in real trouble if they could find her. But they couldn't, so there you were.

Chiffon walked away, slipping through crowds of returning homeowners. She was not hanging around to be accused of abandoning a child so he could burn to death.

It doesn't matter, she reminded herself. Elony was there.

Grass Canyon Road
4:20 P.M.

Wendy Severyn stared at the fire.

It had finished its job on this stretch of road.

Where firefighters walked, ash and fire rose up behind them like hot shadows. People had already returned to their destroyed neighborhood, weeping at the solitary standing chimney where once they had had a home, or stunned and rejoicing because the fire had leapfrogged and the zinnia still bloomed and the cat was fine.

Wendy was on Grass, two miles north of Pinch Canyon Road and as unlikely to get there by car as her husband was from several miles south. Traffic wasn't traffic; it wasn't moving. Cars had to move to qualify as traffic.

Wendy Severyn was in excellent shape. She ran mile after mile on the treadmill at the health club. She could abandon the car and run to Pinch. She was so carbound in her thinking that using feet had not previously crossed her mind. Leaving her car was frightening. It was her world, her safety zone, her climate control, her freedom.

Since she liked to be prepared for any occasion, however, she had her gym bag in the car. She changed into running shoes (she had paid more for them than she paid the housekeeper in a week), drove up over a sidewalk, abandoned the car alongside some brick building, strapped on her cellular phone, and started running.

Running up Grass Canyon Road, which climbed slowly and steadily into the hills, was the most exhausting sweaty thing she had ever undertaken in her life. She felt healed, as if she were most of the way into some twelve-step program. Her heart was racing, her lungs gasping, her thighs stabbing with pain, but she was on her way to save her children and that was good.

In ten minutes, she'd run to where traffic was traffic again, weaving, pressing, honking, cutting ahead, drivers staring madly and blindly at some invisible safe spot.

Her throat and lungs hurt and no matter how deeply she breathed, she couldn't get enough air. She wondered if fire could literally burn off the oxygen in the air.

One of us will find the children, she thought. She wanted it to be her. She had a wonderful vision of herself as heroine: lovely and strong and full of lifesaving abilities. How Beau would admire her.

"Help me," said somebody.

Wendy Severyn did not want to break her rhythm, and did not glance at the speaker.

"Please! Help me."

A hand closed over Wendy Severyn's arm. She was furious at this trespass of her space. She turned to shake it off and tell the person where to go, but it was some burn victim. Its gender and age were unclear, its clothes singed and torn, its hair and eyebrows burned off. Wendy Severyn gagged.

"I need medical help," said the thing.

She did not want to be the one.

She looked wildly around for another rescuer. Some official, some person with training, some Good Samaritan type who liked doing this kind of thing.

But the chaos around her had solidified into a nightmare stream of vehicles and humans coming and going on missions of their own and she felt as if she could hunt for hours and nobody would turn to help.

It wrapped its fingers around her forearm and the fingers were all ooky and blackened and somehow wet and oozing.

She was afraid. She didn't know any first aid. She didn't want to touch it and she didn't want it to touch her either.

I can't be stopping to help every person who should have gotten out in time! she thought. I have to get home!

She shook the hand off her arm, with the thought that she was glad Beau had not seen her do that.

Beau.

What if Beau were hurt? Would a stranger stop and help Beau? Or would the stranger shake him off and continue on his own errand?

Wendy Severyn sat down on the edge of the road. She got up again very fast, dusting her fanny, feeling like the idiot of the century. How many people literally sat down in hot coals? She blushed. She was going to display proof of her stupidity until she had a chance to change clothes.

Assuming she still had a house and a closet.

"Okay," she said to the burn victim, "okay," as if this would make things okay and give her a plan. "I passed fire trucks down below us," she said, "so, okay, we'll go back down there and find doctors."

"I can't walk."

Wendy Severyn could not carry this person. This was an adult. She began knocking on the hoods of passing cars, crying out, shouting for people to stop and take a passenger.

Nobody paid any attention. It wasn't that they turned her down, it was that terror had given them their own agendas, and they couldn't really focus on Wendy Severyn.

She had a sudden vision of her own little girl, knocking endlessly on her parents' lives, but they never saw, and never stopped, and never paid attention.

Pinch Canyon Road
4:21 P.M.

Hall would have to drive right over fire.

Branches had been hurled by the tornado of the fire into the street, and were burning in his path.

What happened to cars driving through fire? What happened to the gas in the tank? What happened to the passengers in the car? Should he have the windows down, in which case fire and burning wind could come through, or up, in which case they would get so hot inside the car they would poach? Should he try running the air-conditioning on an engine so hot he was afraid to place another demand on it?

"Okay, guys, hang on." He put the pedal to the metal, relying on speed as his only defense, and drove over flame. Either the undersides of cars were not bothered by fire after all, or the Suburban was a really great car. In any event they hurtled to the mouth of Pinch Canyon, the fire behind them, safety in front of them — and the gate was closed.

Nobody sat in the little guardhouse.

Nobody stood waiting to swing the wide gate and give them a little wave.

Hall had actually expected Alan Davey to stay with his job, had actually expected him to help at this stage. But that was absurd. Of course any halfway sane person would be long gone. Mr. Davey had a tiny little color TV in the guardhouse, and probably had been paying attention, as Danna and Hall had not, to local warnings.

Part of the guard's job was to use a special allhouse warning system on the phone monitor. The phones are out, Hall remembered. Luckily, the Severyns kept the magnetic gate card under

a little strap on the visor, and Hall yanked it
down and swiped it through the little slot to
open the gate.

It failed.

He ran it through again. And a third time.

The gate did not open.

Cool, said Hall to himself.

His sister moaned; Elisabeth whispered, "No,
no, no, no, no," and Elony was praying in Spanish. There seemed no point in consulting with
anybody back there.

High canyon walls gave him very little vision.
Smoke made it hard to gauge whether there was
a safety zone ahead or not. He wondered where
Egypt and Spice were. He felt sick about the
horses.

"Stupid gate," muttered Hall. He jumped out,
casting a desperate look behind him. No flames
yet. He raced to open the gate by hand.

It would not open.

Hall couldn't believe it.

Then he remembered that that was the point
of having a gate: to stop people from opening it.

It must unlock from the guardhouse.

Slow feet lifted through slow time. Swollen
brain and fat fingers struggled to accomplish any
task at all.

I'm panicking, he thought. I cannot panic. Nobody can help but me. This is my job. Period.
Do not panic.

It helped to admit that he was panicking. Sort

of like AA, he thought, where it helped to admit you were a drunk.

Good evening. My name is Halstead Press and I've panicked, he said to an invisible meeting, and grinned to himself.

The guardhouse itself was locked.

What — did Mr. Davey think somebody would loot the guardhouse? Take his little TV?

In the pretty little beds of flowers beyond the gate, he saw the unmistakable tracks of horses. They'd figured out how to get around. So Hall certainly ought to be able to, too. He kicked in the door of the guardhouse, unlocked the gate from the inside, opened the gate with another kick — kicks were so satisfying — and leaped back in the Suburban. The size and weight of the vehicle made him realize that the gate was actually just a toy: He could have barreled through like a stunt driver, and the Suburban would have been fine, would have carried the gate on its bumper like a Christmas wreath.

Everybody — Danna, Elisabeth, Elony, and Geoffrey — sighed with relief when Hall was back and driving.

He loved that.

He loved that they needed him, that they were afraid without him, that they had no savior but Hall himself.

I'm the hero, thought Hall, and he was stunned and proud.

the Severyn house
4:21 P.M.

The house stank evilly, every shred of Dacron, Orlon, rayon, polyester, and Teflon emitting poisons as they melted or burned. Beau came in through the front door, which was wide open. The wind swooshed through, and Beau so completely misunderstood what wind and fire did together that he was grateful for the breeze. He jogged into the living room, which was intact, in a filthy sort of way: It looked preburned. Gray, but not charred.

He grabbed the cardboard box with such vigor and relief that he crushed the box and the ashes began to fall out. He yanked his shirt up like an apron to contain the box bottom and grinned. He'd done it. And the driveway wasn't that bad. He could get back down it and though he couldn't catch up to the Suburban, he bet he could outrun the fire.

The house sucked in oxygen like a kid with a straw in the bottom of the milk shake.

Beau seized the couch blanket, the one that Lizzie liked to wrap up in, claiming the air-conditioning was too cold for sitting still. The water still flowed in the kitchen faucet, so he soaked the blanket — and then fire jumped out of the walls. It licked him and his box.

He looked down at his arms and fire was resting on them.

He jerked away, but the fire rested on his pant legs.

Smoke came, but separately, somehow, like a second enemy.

Go back out the front door, he told himself, and he lurched toward the big main room. It surprised him that his fine strong reliable legs were not doing very well. He needed great gulps of air, but when he took great gulps there was no oxygen in it, and he felt his head puffing and yet condensing. Felt himself losing brain and thought.

The smoke closed in: filthy, oily, disgusting smoke, coating his face and his lips and his tongue and his throat and the inside of his lungs.

Fire rose up in front of him, filling the living room where it was impossible for flames to be, because the floor was tile, it couldn't burn.

He whirled like the fire: the two of them in a dance before they met as permanent partners.

His shoelaces were blackening. He could not tell if they were starting to burn, or if the smoke had coated them.

His chest hurt in a way unrelated to heart or muscle.

I'm dying in my lungs, he thought. I'll die on the inside before I burn on the outside.

For Michael, it had been the reverse: AIDS had taken him on the outside, destroying his body, but leaving his mind and the ability to feel pain right there. Or so Beau guessed. He was a closet

AIDS-reader. He read everything he could find on it, trying to be where his unknown brother had been. And everything he read was so hideous. It was such a vicious disease. Your body rotted without letting your soul go.

Beau needed to get out of the house.

Now.

But he could not discern the outlines of the room.

Where there should have been a door, there was solid flatness, and where there should have been a wall, there was empty stretching space. He was lost in the smoke of his own house.

Or his own mind.

What am I doing here? he thought.

Had this master plan of foolishness — taking Michael to safety — been percolating in his mind ever since the box arrived on the mantel?

Or was it lack of oxygen and panic coalescing like a chem lab experiment gone bad?

This wasn't Michael, this box. Wherever Michael was, he wasn't in this box. And Dad — whatever Dad hoped for, keeping that box there — Dad wasn't going to find it in a box. And Beau — whatever he needed to know about why his father had abandoned his firstborn but was good to his second-born — Beau was only going to learn that by asking his father.

Michael, thought Beau, I've done something really stupid.

Heat was on all sides. Smoke had hidden the

escape routes, if there were any. Lack of oxygen had absorbed his thoughts, and the sneakers he kept trying to lift kept not lifting.

There had to be a way out.

Of course, there was no way out of AIDS. In trying to discover his brother, was Beau just following him?

People would find his body. They would try to figure out what he had been doing, where he had been going. Would they stand there, some official committee, plus his mother and father, shaking their heads and saying, "Kids. They're so dumb. What did he think would happen?"

He didn't want to die stupid.

He didn't want to die.

He saw himself quite plainly in that fraction of a second: a strong young man standing still, doing nothing, waiting for the fire to take him.

I'm not trying, he thought, and was stunned by this discovery.

But it took oxygen to try anything, and Beau had none left.

Pinch Canyon gate
4:22 P.M.

From way up and way behind the Suburban came a huge tearing screaming sound. Like an avalanche. Hall pressed the gas down harder, and looked up into the rear view mirror, peering through the grime of the back windshield to see what enemy was chasing them now.

Fire had burned away the underpinnings of the Severyn deck, and some of the house. The house had actually ripped, or burned, in half, and was falling down the steep sheer drop into the canyon rock below.

ARMED
RESPONSE

Pinch Canyon
4:24 P.M.

Elony had found in life that it is best not to look.

Don't look back, don't look to the sides, sometimes don't even look ahead, just go blind.

Elony herself looked mainly down at Danna, who was not coping well with agony. Elony had been in agony a time or two but she hadn't screamed and cried like this.

Elisabeth was also sobbing, which Elony certainly understood. If her big brother had run back into a burning building, she would have wept also. Elony rather liked Beau, since he so often gave her a ride to the bus stop. She was sorry that he was a fool.

She scooped Elisabeth into her arms. How willingly the little girl came. As if arms were things she dreamed of and Elisabeth was always on the lookout for arms. "Your brother will be all right," said Elony. "God will take care of him."

"Really?" whispered Elisabeth.

"All he has to do is ask." Her English had arrived! Sort of like a bus, coming on time for once. Elony was amazed and proud.

"I'm not sure Beau would ask God for anything," said Elisabeth nervously.

Really, she was a plain little thing. Elony felt sorry for her. These were the beautiful people. You had to have so much personality to overcome being plain among the beautiful. "Then *we* will ask, you and I," said Elony, "and God will still hear."

Elony was not certain that God paid attention to barbaric languages, so she prayed in Spanish.

Pinch Canyon
4:24 P.M.

Pine trees swayed so much in the updrafts they looked as if they were planning to run away. The fire climbed them in seconds, almost faster than you could count. The cones were a different color fire from the bark and the needles: For a moment each cone was scarlet, like a Christmas tree bulb.

Halstead Press could not get over the magnificence of it — and the extent of it. Where did it end? When would he come out? Were they caught in some reverse tunnel in which everything was light and fire, and nothing was dark, unlit, and safe?

He was not great at steering, nor braking, nor accelerating.

It was clear that these things took practice,

and should not be taken up by individuals fleeing fire. The steering wheel was not at the right angle for Hall, and the floor pedals seemed far too large for human feet, as if the car designer had had a Yeti in mind.

When Hall was eight, he'd gotten into drag racing and spent lots of time on a track, but he lost interest before he was ten, to his father's sorrow, because this was a father/son activity if there ever was one. Actual car driving, in actual normal-sized cars (not that the Suburban was normal — it was like driving a tank) Hall had never done.

The fine smooth roads of California turned out to be full of bumps and dips. Each bump and dip was accompanied by a cry of pain from Danna.

The adrenaline in him made Hall a different person. In spite of his inexperience and fear, he was extremely confident. Confidence filled him, topped him, he was overflowing with certainty that he knew what he was doing and would pull it off. In only a few hundred yards, another minor fire to skirt, another deep canyon drop-off not to go off, and they would emerge onto Grass Canyon Road where ARMED RESPONSE would be there to welcome him and set Danna's leg.

It was at this profound moment that the kittens finally broke out of their cardboard. Within seconds Kumquat, Lemon, and Orange were everywhere; it felt as if there were twenty or thirty kittens, on the dashboard, on his shoulder, under the gas pedal. "Elisabeth!" he yelled. "Get the kittens!"

"How?" asked Elisabeth reasonably.

I'm a stuntman in a movie about vacations for insane people, thought Hall.

Geoffrey was actually exhibiting excitement. He hopped up and down, seat belt long gone, and silence a thing of the past. "Lookit, lookit!"

Hall scooped a kitten out from under the accelerator and then looked. A cactus, the fat-armed spiny type, was filled by heat like an air balloon. Suddenly it deflated, and the cactus sagged down on itself like a dead thing. "I see it, Geoffrey!" Hall honked the horn, in honor of the cactus and Geoffrey's speech.

the Severyn house
4:24 P.M.

Beau had made it to the atrium when the house split in half.

It shook the ground like the earthquakes they so often felt. It fell too slowly for reality, its beams hanging on, its bolts not yielding. But gravity was stronger.

The smoke lifted momentarily. All around him the fire was savage and terrible. But on the canyon rim, the fire had burned itself out. The top of the hills were burned and black and dead.

If he wanted to live, Beau had to pass *through* the flames and up to where the flames were no more. Pinch Canyon above the Severyn house was very steep. He couldn't run up. He could only crawl. Pinch had nothing to hold onto. Its gravel, dried mud, dead weeds, and rocks looked solid, but came off in the hand.

It was so hot now the soles of his sneakers were melting.

Don't think, just go, he told himself. And if you die, remember Michael is there waiting.

Well, that wasn't rational. Michael wasn't anywhere waiting. Michael just plain wasn't.

He draped the sopping blanket over himself, cuddled the box to his chest as if it were an ally and not a burden, and began.

The noise increased. Beau was beneath the landing patterns of jets or standing at the juncture of freight trains. The noise was immense and encompassing and he could not get away from it, yet he could not see the fire making this immense sound.

The air was literally hung with soot. Would his lungs endure ten seconds or thirty seconds or sixty seconds before they disobeyed him and took the last great sucking breath that would kill him with its heat and its poison?

the studio
4:24 P.M.

"I wonder where the fires are right now," said Mrs. Press.

"I don't know," said Mr. Press, "but it's nothing to do with us. Danna or Hall would have phoned if there was anything to worry about."

the Severyn house
4:25 P.M.

There had been quite a while, twenty minutes, maybe even half an hour, in which the fire had struggled. Eaten a little here, a little there. That was over. Something — the gas line, probably — had given it the strength of war.

Nature was all: sheets of fire ten or a hundred feet high, the fury of the fire whipping through the narrow slot of Pinch like an angry spouse hurling plates.

Beau held the box in his teeth and crawled up the rock, and it was so hot it burned the skin off his palms but that sort of thing didn't matter anymore; what mattered was the top, the crest, the hill.

Getting the car and Elisabeth out had been a narcotic: He'd been drugged with joy at finding out he was brave and did the right things. And so he had moved past that, thinking he would be even braver and better and finally superior.

But he wasn't.

He was dumb and he was trapped.

He clung to the cardboard box, although its contents had already burned once and could not burn again, but would just blend in with the deaths of trees and houses and Beau.

Beau had lots and lots of time for thinking, even though he had very very little time left for living.

The bear went over the mountain, thought Beau, singing the nursery rhyme in his head, knowing that he was becoming confused; he was sinking. *The bear went over the mountain, to see what he could see. The other side of the mountain, the other side of the mountain . . .*

That can't be all, thought Beau. There has to be more there than just the other side of the mountain. There has to be safety.

And water.

Please.

Pacific Coast Highway
4:25 P.M.

Swann's mother was elated.

They had some fabulous jewelry. Some great silver. A really incredibly gorgeous thing, they did not know what it was, cut-edged crystal, glittering with diamonds. And even more albums. The Eight-Car family had spent their lives taking pictures of each other.

The photograph albums they threw in the street.

Laughing, they drove back toward their motel.

"Great state," said Swann's dad.

"I love California," agreed Swann's mom.

The highway patrol officer who pulled them over also thought California was a great state. He thought it was very interesting that people would toss the photographs for which they had just risked their lives. He thought it was real interesting that tourists wearing obscene T-shirts were bedecked in pearls and diamonds. He thought maybe they needed to talk about this.

"It wasn't me," said Swann quickly. "It was them."

Grass Canyon Road
4:26 P.M.

It was actually a very short drive.

Hall had thought he would journey for hours, but it was barely even minutes, because he turned left on Grass, and in a quarter of a mile, hit the great line of fire trucks and firefighters.

It was another world here, because of all the officials. Such a reassuring beautiful world: vivid red and neon yellow and ice white vehicles of safety and rescue. All those people in their yellow fire-resistant outfits. All those adults.

Hall sort of expected a brass band or a television interview, certainly a round of applause.

But through traffic and smoke and confusion and fear, nobody noticed the addition of another vehicle, even when that vehicle was coming from the fire side.

Here the land opened up, and he could see the horizons, the fire visible in the hills. Soaring black and orange in the sky, Halloween colors, the fire seemed a very distant enemy. Hall had learned the hard way that distance was deceiving, and yet immediately he believed in it again.

In this area, a mild fire had already passed through. Beside the Suburban was a row of palm trees like diamond-sided telephone poles, with tiaras of graceful leaves. Every one was black. No leaves remained. The fire had eaten only the skin, lost interest, and passed on.

The beautiful land was desolate and terribly ugly. It was hard to look at anything very long.

In the driveway next to where Hall parked, there must have been a garage, but now there was absolutely nothing but a Sears Craftsman toolbox, no longer red, bent in the middle like a cheap wire clothes hanger, its little drawer knobs melted.

"We made it!" yelled Geoffrey.

His little failure-to-thrive neighbor was thriving. Enjoying himself. Talking and waving.

Maybe he just needed action, thought Hall.

Maybe it was all that sitting at home. This is a guy who needs to be out in the world.

Hall could hardly wait to tell Mr. and Mrs. Aszling about the transformation. He was already full of plans for how to teach the Aszlings to be better parents, not that they had been interested in Hall's suggestions before. But they would be now, and now that he was a hero, and had rescued the whole neighborhood, he'd have clout and they'd —

But it was not the Aszlings he recognized through the chaos.

It was Mr. Severyn, hopping down off a huge flatbed trailer that carried an immense yellow bulldozer, waving good-bye as casually as if leaving the airport after a routine flight. He wore a suit but not a tie, and looked as if he had a meeting scheduled here in the fireplace of Grass Canyon.

There would be meetings.

But not with Beau.

Los Angeles General Hospital
4:27 P.M.

Matt Marsh was turning the hospital sheets black from his ash. He wasn't in pain; they'd medicated him pretty heavily; it was a strange loopy feeling and he didn't know why he wasn't asleep. Perhaps he was asleep and couldn't tell.

I made a real save, he thought. An honest-to-God, lifesaving save.

He wondered what that meant — honest to God. And he decided that he had been honest with God, and God had been honest with him.

"Darling, you must quit now," said Matt Marsh's mother, horrified by his wrecked face, kissing his sooty hair. "Surely you see now how dangerous and terrible it is to be a firefighter."

Matt Marsh loved his mother. He even loved how little she understood.

I was brave enough.

I moved fast enough.

I am good enough.

"Mom," he said, smiling through the burns, "try to understand. It was great. I'd do it again in a hot second."

Grass Canyon Road
4:27 P.M.

I'm not a hero, thought Hall. He deflated like the heat-killed cactus. I let Beau go. I let him go without even a fight.

And now I have to tell his father . . . Hi, well, at least I got one of them, but the other one? The boy? He was nice while he lasted, but these things happen, Mr. Severyn, you win some, you burn some.

It sickened Hall that even in this, he started and finished flippant.

Halstead Press swallowed, and his tongue was dry and painful on his cracking lips. He looked at Elisabeth, who had seen her father, and was staring at him with a sort of deep apprehension. She didn't call out either.

The ways in which he had failed hit Hall like a slug in the jaw.

"It wasn't your fault, Elisabeth," said Hall. He couldn't even use Beau's name. The name, like Beau, was probably over. "It was my fault. Your father won't be mad at you."

"Mr. Severyn," he called finally, because he was the oldest here. He, for better or for worse, was in charge.

He knew right away that Mr. Severyn did not recognize him. They were that kind of parent. "I'm Halstead Press, I live down the road from you. I have Elisabeth."

"Of course," said Mr. Severyn, and he opened the door of the Suburban and closed his eyes with relief and lifted his little girl onto his shoulder. "Oh, honey! You're black from smoke. Your pant leg is burned off! Are you all right?"

Mr. Severyn did not appear to notice that Elisabeth's legs had been straddling a sobbing Danna on the car floor. He did not even glance at the other three occupants of the back of the Suburban. What does that mean? thought Hall.

Elisabeth's father stroked the black streaks on

his daughter's cheeks and arms. "You've been crying," he said, kissing her tear stains. "Everything's okay now, honey." He hugged her hard, and hugged her again, and with each squeeze Elisabeth looked safer and better. "You're okay," crooned her father. "You got out. Now where's Beau?"

Grass Canyon Road
4:27 P.M.

"I know you!" cried Wendy Severyn, grabbing at Chiffon's blackened clothing.

I'm caught, thought Chiffon. They're going to know now that I abandoned the baby. She felt as sick as if Mrs. Severyn had put handcuffs on her. She felt as sick as if she were entering a women's prison. She tried to think of a way to lie, to extricate herself from this, but nothing came to mind.

Mrs. Severyn was the most beautiful of the beautiful people, even in sweat, even in smoke. But she wasn't quite sure who Chiffon was. "Aren't you — I think — don't you work for somebody in Pinch Canyon? What's happening? Where are my children?"

She doesn't know me, thought Chiffon, elated, hopeful. Smoke wafted around them, like a scarf, but you could not take smoke off. Chiffon looked around for an escape route, and saw one. "Over there!" she pointed. "Look! There they are. I lost them in the smoke."

She grabbed Mrs. Severyn's shoulders and pointed her toward the Suburban, in whose window, amazingly, Geoffrey stood, and in front of whose doors, amazingly, Mr. Severyn hugged Elisabeth.

"Thank God!" breathed Mrs. Severyn. "You take care of this burned person. He needs an ambulance. I'm sure there's one somewhere." Mrs. Severyn transferred a crispy hand into Chiffon's and rushed over to the Suburban.

The hand clenched Chiffon's in pain, and she recoiled in horror. The burn had left the hand literally toasted, dry and hard as if you should spread butter on it.

Chiffon yelled for a firefighter, and this time one of them came. She transferred the crispy fingers to his glove, and he took them, and knelt beside the creature, and Chiffon beat it. This was why you paid taxes, to have people around to do the ooky things, and Chiffon herself was done with ooky things.

She had some of Mr. Aszling's money in her purse, and if she hurried she could get to an ATM to draw out the rest of her own money, and then she was hitting the road. Coming up with a good excuse for leaving Geoffrey was beyond her, and the thing to do was get beyond punishment. Now.

Grass Canyon Road
4:28 P.M.

Wendy Severyn's first, and most terrible thought, was that she did not have to feel guilty after all. The difficult child was okay, and she did not have to lie awake the rest of her life wondering if she should have done something else. Her husband still held Elisabeth, so all Wendy had to do was peck her on the cheek. For form's sake, she said, "Elisabeth, darling, you're all right."

All Elisabeth wanted to know was whether she could have a kitten. It seemed to Wendy Severyn that every conversation with Elisabeth was like this — pointless and nothing to do with anything. The world was on fire and Elisabeth wanted a pet?

"Yes, you may have a kitten," she said, because what did it matter now? Then she got to the point. "Where's Beau?"

The car was very quiet.

Even the fire and the vehicles and the volunteers seemed to get quiet for that question.

Elisabeth said nothing.

Danna on the floor said nothing.

Halstead Press said nothing.

Nothing. It was the worst thing in the world, that the only answer about your beloved son was *nothing*.

"*Where's Beau?*" screamed Wendy Severyn.

Grass Canyon Road
4:28:30 P.M.

It was wonderful to be standing next to official
vehicles. The bright colors, immense letters,
crackle of radios, the piles of equipment — so
reassuring. Elony loved America that way, the
way they had so *much* stuff. The way they
hurled themselves at things, always believing
they could conquer anything, even nature.

In the huge outside rearview mirror Elony saw
herself black with smoke. She stank. Fire
smelled bad and so did its victims.

She was grateful to Beau for bringing the Suburban down to the road before he became a fool
and went back into the fire. She was grateful to
Hall for driving them out. She had a debt. And
nobody would get mad at her for telling the
truth.

She said in her surprising new English, "Beau
went back into the fire. Back into the house.
Even though it had fire. We couldn't wait for
him. The house burned. It fell off the canyon."

Grass Canyon Road
4:29 P.M.

Beau's father had never had an employee ca-
pable of delivering such a succinct message. It

was very well done, that summary of Elony's. It included everything except the conclusion.

Beau's death.

Mr. Severyn turned to stare at the hills of sphinxes that were the rims of many canyons. They were dark and kept their secrets. "No," he whispered numbly. "What would he do that for? He'd gotten out! And gotten Elisabeth out! Why would he go back?"

Nobody answered him.

"No!" screamed Mrs. Severyn. "He has to be all right." She left running and shrieking, pounding on the shoulders of firefighters, telling them that her son was in danger, they had to go now, and save her son. Nothing else mattered.

How clearly the words rang in the sooty air.

Nothing else mattered.

Elisabeth had known that, but until now, she had had hope.

Her father stood very still and very silent. He had to close his eyes to stay inside his thoughts instead of running screaming after Wendy. There was absolutely nothing in that house that Beau had cared enough about to go back for.

Except . . .

Could one brother really have died to save the ashes of the other? It was too hideous.

Aden Severyn felt like a character in an ancient Greek tragedy. There was no escape from the dreadful darkness of fate. Fate came.

Just because I was a lousy father to Michael,

he said to Beau, doesn't mean anything. I needed
space back then. I wasn't ready to be a parent.
I had to give myself room. And Michael placed
unfair demands on me. And when he died . . .

"If Beau is dead," said Mr. Severyn dully, "it's
my fault." He found that he was still holding
Elisabeth. He tried to figure out where they
were, how they had gotten there, what he should
do next.

"No," said Hall. "It's Beau's fault. It isn't anybody's fault but Beau's."

Grass Canyon Road
4:29:30 P.M.

"Okay, sweetie," said the fireman, smiling
down at Danna. All she could think of was pain-
killers. Would he give her something? She didn't
have to wait to reach the hospital, did she?

They were doing things to her broken leg that
Danna didn't want to watch, and she desperately
didn't want to scream, either. Mrs. Severyn was
screaming for a dead son, so how could Danna
do exactly the same thing? Steal that cry? Use
up a scream on a mere bone?

She had heard of Wailing Walls in Israel, and
she heard Mrs. Severyn standing at her own
Wailing Wall, the place where you screamed in
helplessness for the dead you wanted back.

And they didn't come back. Beau was not coming back. Danna hoped it had not hurt for Beau. If a broken leg hurt like this, what had burning up hurt like?

The act of not screaming took up the energy she had left, and it felt as if her rescuers were sliding somebody else onto the stretcher; lifting somebody else into the back of the helicopter. Her head felt detached, as if her vertebrae had come undone. She was bobbling around like a Barbie doll whose owner hadn't stuck the head on all the way.

Danna wanted to call good-bye to her brother, congratulate him, thank him, be proud of him, but rescue was like fire: When it came, it came so fast. You could only hold on; you couldn't do anything yourself.

"It's okay, sweetie," said the fireman again, "we're just giving you some medication," but this time he was somebody else; a helicopter pilot, a different uniform.

"It's okay, sweetie," they said and the door slammed and the copter lifted up with a sickening swerve and a ferocious noise.

It's okay for me, thought Danna. It's okay for Elisabeth and Hall and Geoffrey and Elony. But is it okay for Beau? Are you okay in death?

Oh, Beau! Why did you do that? Did you sort of want that to happen, or did you completely not want it to happen? Did you try to change your mind and couldn't?

Grass Canyon Road
4:30 P.M.

"It's okay?" said Geoffrey nervously, staring way up at Mr. Severyn's face.

Mr. Severyn tried to imagine any world at all now, let alone one which he could call okay.

The inferno was more distant. It was again traveling with the wind, but the other direction. Fire trucks were shifting their war positions. In only a few minutes, they could probably actually walk back into Pinch Canyon, and see what was left.

What a quick world fire was.

Mr. Severyn picked Geoffrey up, remembering Michael at four, Beau at four, Elisabeth at four. "It's okay." His throat was thick with hope. Beau was too good, too smart, too beautiful, too much his son to be dead.

the studio
4:35 P.M.

"Well, that's a wrap!" said Jill Press with delight. "We'll be home for dinner after all. What do you think the kids would like? I'm in the mood for some of that wonderful goat cheese ravioli we had the other day."

"Danna doesn't like it. We could bring them pizza."

They walked slowly out to their cars, sorry they had not driven together, because they were in the mood to keep talking. Jill Press got in her car while her husband continued to discuss the dinner issue through the car window. She'd left her radio on. "Fires continue in Greater Los Angeles," said the news.

"I'm sick of these dumb fires!" She punched the radio button and turned it off. "There!" she said, grinning at her husband. "So much for fire."

Grass Canyon Road
4:55 *P.M.*

Elony was pleased with how well everybody was behaving. It was good that you couldn't classify everybody in the same category as Chiffon or Mr. or Mrs. Aszling. That would reduce your faith in people.

"Ice cream truck!" cried Elony, pointing. Only in America. The ice cream trucks, the taco trucks, the hot dog and soda trucks — you never had to wait long. She smiled at Mr. Severyn. "You pay," she explained.

He nodded. "I pay." And somehow they were all standing around having toasted almond and orange Creamsicle and chocolate cherry dip.

Elony felt desperately sorry for the man. It was a new experience, to be better off than Californians were. She had already buried her family, and her history too. Someday the father would smile again, and someday the mother would laugh. Someday Elisabeth would forget and someday the sky would be blue and clean again. Without Beau.

Nature never needed anybody. It went on by itself, following its own rules.

Elony was thinking in English. She felt almost reverent, that her mind had pulled it off.

"Daddy, I think we should adopt Geoffrey," said Elisabeth. "Elony would come, too, and we'd all live happily ever after." She had bought vanilla ice cream in a cup for the kittens to lick.

"Mr. and Mrs. Aszling love Geoffrey," said Mr. Severyn, which wasn't true, and they all knew it wasn't true, but which he felt compelled to say anyhow. They looked at him and he flushed and occupied himself licking his ice cream.

"But Elony could live with us," he said. Companionship for his daughter, a safe easy baby-sitter.

He glanced at Elony and was shocked to see such relief on her face, the relief of a child who is about to be taken care of after all; and he saw now that Elony *was* a child, not just help, and that she, like Elisabeth, needed shelter and love. *We'd all live happily ever after.* What else did anybody ever want?

He had no idea where he had been in his life,

nor where he was going, but he knew at least that the fire had given instruction and he'd better pay attention.

He could see part of Pinch Mountain. The barren slope twitched as if it possessed nerve endings. A little branch full of pine sap exploded and gusts of wind made ash devils.

He could see officials approaching, and knew that they were coming to him. He could read in their bodies the dread with which they walked forward.

When they said quietly and carefully that they had found Beau, he knew they did not mean Beau alive.

Happily ever after, he thought. Both my sons! It can't be, I can't take it, I cannot go on without them.

He was vaguely aware of his screaming, sobbing wife, vaguely aware that tranquilizers were decided upon for her, and then an ambulance.

After a long time, he saw that he still had a daughter, and he tried to think of something to say. The only thing he could come up with was, "I love you, honey."

When he saw how badly she had needed to hear that, he wondered how much Michael or Beau might have liked to hear it, but it was too late for them.

Grass Canyon Road
4:55 P.M.

Hall wanted his parents so bad he could hardly manage not to scream, the way Mrs. Severyn had screamed. If he had lost one of his family . . .

He imagined them in their cars, engulfed by hundred-foot flames. He imagined them in their cars, breathing in a solid wall of black smoke. Turning to charred, dead, stinking flesh.

The once beautiful California hills encircled him like a black soiled wreath. The land twitched, erupting here and there with flame or a burst of smoke or a sizzle of sparks. Dead houses and corpses of cars were just litter.

His own house was gone. His entire neighborhood was gone. Beau, short for beautiful, was dead. Fire was stronger than people, even the beautiful people.

And what if fire had been stronger than Hall's mother and father? Hall didn't exactly pray. He built a wall out of a single word, a wall of brick repeats: *no, no, no, no, no, no, no.*

Exhaustion hit Hall. He did not see how he could stand up any longer, or form another syllable, or lift another eyelid.

They had taken Danna so suddenly, so completely. Just whisked her away, as if she were *their* sister instead of his. He knew he could trust them, but to have her flown off into the ashy sky without him — it left him with nothing. Nobody.

They had said Hall could go with her, but Hall could not go; he had to take care of the neighborhood. Mr. Severyn was managing for a minute, but that would end. In a minute, Mr. Severyn would understand what had happened to his son. He would look at the remains of hills and houses and know that was also the remains of Beau.

If only I'd fought with Beau, Hall wept in his heart. If only I'd knocked him down. Forced him back into the car. If only I could do it differently.

He rubbed tears with his fists, like a grubby little kindergartner.

So terrible, to find out that the best you could do might not be much.

He watched Elisabeth, savoring any crumb of affection her father gave her. She was as damaged as Geoffrey, her landscape as bleak as if she, too, had grown up unloved in a silent orphanage.

And then, unmarred by smoke or fire, his mother's car nosed its way through the press of rescue vehicles and tourists and television crews and neighbors. Then his father's car, right behind her. Hall's parents vaulted out from behind their steering wheels, eyes wide with horror, heads swiveling for clues, hearts falling with fear.

He knew exactly what brick wall against fate the single word was building in their hearts and mouths: *no, no, no, no, no, no!* Not Hall. Not Danna. Please, take our house, take land, take anything we've ever owned, but spare our children.

There was nothing on earth more wonderful than parents who loved you. Hall had them. Danna had them.

"Mom," he croaked, trying to walk toward them, but he was sapped of all strength. They would have to come to him. "Dad."

They saw him. They ran.

"We're all right," he said. "We made it."

ABOUT THE AUTHOR

Caroline B. Cooney lives in a small seacoast village in Connecticut, with thousands of books and two pianos. She writes every day on a word processor and then goes for a long walk down the beach to figure out what she's going to write the following day. She has written over fifty books for young people, including *The Party's Over*, *The Face on the Milk Carton*, *Whatever Happened to Janie?*, and *Flight #116 Is Down*, which was selected as an ALA Recommended Book for the Reluctant YA Reader.

MED CENTER

**A building blows up . . .
and Med Center's volunteers
feel the shock waves.**

It's bad enough that Med Center is crowded
with victims of a chemical explosion. But
worse yet, many of the wounded are still
trapped inside the building. Is it worth it for
the Med Center volunteers to risk their lives
in a dangerous rescue attempt?

BLAST

MED CENTER #4
BY DIANE HOH

**Their lives are nonstop drama . . .
inside the hospital and out.**

Coming soon to a bookstore near you.

MC396

Every day
Sara Howell
faces mystery,
danger... and silence.

Sara is being followed, and the stalker knows her every move...

A newspaper headline is altered to read "Deaf Rower Dies"; a single white rose is left without a note; Sara's dress for the dance is mysteriously slashed. Then someone threatens her hearing-ear dog, Tuck. Where can Sara go when the stalker gets closer day after day?

HEAR NO EVIL #3
A Time of Fear
Kate Chester

Coming soon to a bookstore near you.

HNE296